"The — my life hell

What was that? Three muffled figures came out of a side road and stood directly in front of me. They were girls – I was sure of that, they weren't tall enough to be guys – but they had scarves and hats on so I couldn't swear it was anyone I knew. I thought I recognized Meg Tate's black coat . . . and wasn't that Karen Connor's distinctive red hair I could see tucked under a dark-coloured hat?

"What d'you want?" I said more confidently than I felt, as they were blocking my path.

No one said anything.

I tried to walk on, push through them, and then felt a shove in the small of my back that sent me sprawling into the gutter. My school bag went flying and I felt something – a boot, probably – catch my shoulder a glancing blow.

Muggers! I thought as I lay there, terrified, curling my arms round my head to protect it. Oh, no! What are they going to do to me? I haven't got any money.

Other books also available in this series:

"They made my life hell"

Jill Eckersley

■ SCHOLASTIC

Scholastic Children's Books
Commonwealth House, 1–19 New Oxford Street,
London WC1A 1NU, UK
A division of Scholastic Ltd
London ~ New York ~ Toronto ~ Sydney ~ Auckland
Mexico City ~ New Delhi ~ Hong Kong

First published in the UK by Scholastic Ltd, 1999

Copyright © Jill Eckersley, 1999

ISBN 0 439 01223 6

Typeset by Falcon Oast Graphic Art
Printed by Cox and Wyman Ltd, Reading, Berks.

10 9 8 7 6 5 4 3 2 1

Prologue

I never, ever imagined it would turn out like this. When Mum and Dad and I moved to Norfolk from London, we thought it was a chance to start a new life after my brother was killed in a car crash.

Settling into a new school felt strange at first. The others had all known one another for years and I felt like an outsider – especially where Valerie Maxwell and her little clique were concerned. They were the in crowd, no doubt about it.

At first, I wanted to be like them. Well, like Valerie, who is everything I'm not – confident, attractive, popular, a bit of a rebel.

But then I met Craig. We hit it off right from the start. I'd never had a real boyfriend before and Craig was the kind of guy I'd always dreamed of meeting.

And there was Anna, too – warm, steadfast Anna, a true friend. Or so I thought. It was Anna who first told me that Craig was Valerie's ex-boyfriend, but it was Valerie who let me know that she wanted him back.

And that was when it started – the tricks, the sabotage, the sly digs, the bitchy remarks. She tried to break Craig and me up. She tried to ruin my life.

I thought things couldn't possibly get worse, but then they did. Because I had an awful secret, something that I didn't want anyone to know about, but especially not Valerie.

If she found out, she'd have the perfect weapon to destroy me with.

And she'd use it, I knew she would. . .

Chapter 1

I thought I would feel sad when moving day came, but I didn't. Partly, it was because I was too busy. There seemed to be loads of last-minute packing to do after the removal van had left with all our furniture. Dad and I ended up shoving a whole lot of things into the car, any old how, hoping they'd survive the journey without breaking or falling apart.

It was Mum I was worried about. She sat at the bottom of the stairs, with a cup of tea I'd brought her from the café across the street, looking sort of dazed, as if she couldn't quite believe what was happening. Mum and Dad had lived in the same house since before Mark, my brother, was born. Every now and then Dad would squeeze her arm as he went past, or say, "All right, love?"

Mum just nodded.

I tried not to think how she must be feeling. To be

3

truthful, I was trying not to think much at all, except that we were moving to Norfolk, to start a new life. We were putting the past behind us, and starting again. That had to be a good thing, didn't it? After all, what are we leaving behind? I thought rather bitterly. Even our house didn't look like home any more, once the furniture and the pictures and all the everyday clutter had been taken away. It was just a house, a semi like all the others in our street, waiting for another family to move in and turn it into a home.

A happy home, like ours had been until that fateful night, just a few months ago. . .

My brother Mark was always a bit of a tearaway, but that had never stopped me loving him. In fact, when I was little, I hero-worshipped him. He was just two and a half years older than me and always seemed able to do things I couldn't, like climb to the top of the old apple tree in our garden, or whistle through his fingers. He spent ages trying to teach me to do that but I never could master it.

He was a real live wire, always into everything, including trouble. Most of it was just mischief, the sort of things young boys do, but when he reached his teens he did go a bit wild. I know Mum worried sometimes, but Mark could charm the birds out of the trees, as my nan used to say. Anyway, Dad had been the same when he was young, so they didn't make too much fuss when he just messed about at school, truanting sometimes, preferring to hang around the Rec or the shopping centre with his mates.

"He'll settle down, love. Look what happened to me!" Dad would say reassuringly when Mark was late home again, or they got an angry letter from the Head complaining that he'd been bunking off.

"School's boring," Mark would say airily when Dad had a go at him. "What use is it going to be to me, learning a load of soppy poems or history dates?"

"What sort of a job d'you think you're going to get, without any qualifications?" Mum would say.

But Mark only laughed. "I'll be OK, Mum," he'd say confidently. "Trust me."

He left school as soon as he possibly could and got a job selling CDs on a mate's market stall. He was a born salesman with the gift of the gab, so he did brilliantly, and was soon earning really good money.

"Told you so, didn't I?" he'd grin, as he treated Mum to a nice bunch of flowers or took us all out for a meal in another mate's Italian restaurant.

What could we say? I still thought Mark was a fantastic guy, and so did about half the local girls. He was a real heartbreaker, without meaning to be. Deep down he was a big softie and a girl only had to look a bit lost or sad or pathetic and he'd promise her anything. The trouble was, he'd promise her mate anything too. And her mum. And her gran. And the woman sitting next to him on the bus.

By the time I was sixteen I'd got used to being "Mark Gilbert's sister". Sometimes girls tried to get to know me *because* I was Mark's sister, and for a while I didn't even mind that. Unlike my brother I've never found it that easy to make friends. I'm a bit shy, if you want to know the truth – not upfront and confident, like my brother. Eventually I learned to spot the girls who were only trying to make friends with me so they'd have an excuse to hang around Mark. I knew he wasn't looking for a steady girlfriend, so they were wasting their time, and after a bit I learned to laugh at them.

I even helped Mark out sometimes, fielding their telephone calls, telling them he was out when he didn't want to speak to some lovelorn girl. Well, after all, he was my brother. I didn't always approve of the things he did, but I still loved him.

You know, I still can't believe it sometimes, and I don't think Mum and Dad can either. We thought we knew Mark – a charmer, a chancer, a bit of a Jack-the-Lad, but not a criminal. And definitely, *definitely* not a killer. Yet that was just what he turned out to be.

Every detail of that night is etched on to my memory, like one of those awful nightmares that seem to cling to you long after you've woken up.

The first hint of anything wrong came with a ring on the doorbell, about ten o'clock in the evening. Mum and Dad and I were watching TV. I'd just finished my homework. Unlike Mark, I was ambitious and wanted to get good GCSE grades.

"Wonder who that is?" Dad said casually.

"Perhaps Mark's forgotten his key. It wouldn't be the first time," Mum replied.

I was nearest, so I got up to answer the door.

When I saw two policemen standing there, I wasn't especially bothered at first. We'd been having a bit of trouble with local kids spraying graffiti around and trampling on the flower beds, so I thought that was what they'd come about.

"Yes?"

"Miss . . . Gilbert?" said the older of the two.

"Yes?"

"Are your parents in?"

"Well . . . yes, they are but—"

"May we come in?"

Even then I wasn't especially concerned. I called Dad, and opened the living-room door to let the policemen in.

"Mr and Mrs Gilbert? Is your son Mark Gilbert?"

Mum's hand went to her throat and all the colour drained from her face.

"Yes . . . Mark. What's happened? Is he all right?"

The policeman didn't seem able to meet Mum's eyes.

"I'm afraid there's been an accident, Mrs Gilbert," his colleague said gently.

"An accident?" Dad echoed blankly.

"A car crash up on Park Road North."

I saw Dad reach for Mum's hand and hold it tight.

"A Ford Mondeo jumped the lights and crashed into a mini-cab. I'm afraid there were fatalities."

"Fatalities?" said Dad. "Are you telling me my – our son is dead?"

The policeman bowed his head.

"I'm afraid so. I'm very, very sorry."

"But . . . there must be some mistake."

Mum sounded quite calm. She was even smiling.

"I'm sorry, officer, but you're wrong. Mark doesn't drive a Ford Mondeo. He hasn't even got a car. It can't be Mark that's – that's dead, it must be someone else."

The policeman cleared his throat.

"Mr Gilbert . . . Mrs Gilbert . . . believe me, I'm truly sorry to have to tell you this, but . . . we have reason to believe that the Mondeo was being driven without the owner's consent."

There was an awful silence. I couldn't, I just *couldn't* believe what I was hearing.

"You mean . . . Mark was driving a stolen car?" Dad gasped.

The policeman nodded.

That was when I knew – when we all knew – that there was no mistake.

I felt as though my whole world had suddenly turned upside-down, as if this evening was all a horrible, horrible dream, as if I'd wake up at any moment and Mum would be bending over me with a cup of tea, saying, "Kerry? Come on, dormouse, time to get up. School today."

But I knew it wasn't going to happen. Instead I had to sit there, listening to this grave-faced policeman telling me things I didn't want to hear, couldn't bear to hear. Mark, my lovely, laughing, wheeling-and-dealing, life-loving brother, was dead, mangled in the wreckage of a stolen car. His friend Danny Potter, who'd been with him, was on a life-support machine in our local hospital.

And that wasn't the worst of it.

It was only later, when Dad and Mum, looking white and ill and somehow much older, had been up to the hospital to identify Mark's body, that we learned the very worst thing of all.

The car Mark had been driving had spun out of control and crashed into a mini-cab. The driver had escaped with minor injuries, but he'd been carrying two passengers, a woman and her four-year-old daughter. The woman had suffered two cracked ribs and a broken leg.

The little girl, like Mark, had been killed instantly.

I felt as though I was sleepwalking through the next few weeks. I tried not to fall apart, for Mum and Dad's sake, but it was a total nightmare. People were kind at first, but as the story came out – it made a big splash in our local paper – some of our neighbours and people Mum and Dad had counted as friends drifted away. Maybe they didn't know what to say to us. Mark had been a popular guy among his own crowd, but when it came out that he'd stolen a car just for a thrill and driven it so recklessly that he'd killed a four-year-old girl, sympathy somehow dried up.

I thought Mum was going to have a nervous breakdown. I could hear her sobbing in bed at night, after she thought I was asleep. And Dad, who'd always been such a happy-go-lucky guy, rather like Mark, seemed like a shadow of the person he had been.

None of us knew what to say to each other. Mum couldn't even face going into Mark's room and putting his clothes away. My Auntie Cath came in the end and did it for her. Every day, all the time, we felt as though there was something – *someone* – missing. Even the stupidest little things, like setting the table for Sunday lunch for three people instead of four, just about broke my heart.

The crash happened towards the end of the Christmas holidays. Mum and Dad went up to school to talk to the Head and ask if I could have an extra couple of weeks off, in the circumstances, and he said that was OK. School, lessons, exams, going out with my friends, having a laugh – all those things seemed to belong to another world. I couldn't believe I'd ever be able to smile or laugh again.

"You will, Kerry, I'm sure you will," Sue, my best friend, told me. She'd been away at her grand-parents' in Scotland when it all happened, and when she came back she was full of sympathy.

"Mark wouldn't want to think of you all ruining your lives because of him, would he?"

I sniffed. I missed my brother more than I would have believed possible, but I was also mad at him. Now that the numbness was beginning to wear off, I found myself having imaginary conversations with him, asking him how he could possibly have been so stupid. Stealing a car. Joy-riding, they call it. Why? I thought. Why, Mark? Why did you do it? There were plenty of other, legal ways for you to get your kicks. Why did you have to destroy two lives — well, more than two, if you counted mine and Mum's and Dad's as well?

I actually felt quite scared at the idea of going back to school, even though I knew I had to face it — face everyone — one day. I hated the idea of being whispered about, pointed out, as "that girl whose brother was the joy-rider in that car crash — you know, the one where the little girl was killed."

Even if people weren't talking about me, I felt as though they were, which was almost as bad.

I couldn't have faced it without Sue. There were a couple of other girls in my class I was quite friendly with, and they were OK about it. Everyone else seemed to look kind of embarrassed and sidle away whenever I appeared.

"They probably just don't know what to say to you," said Sue. "Nobody's blaming you for what your brother did, Kerry, honest."

But that wasn't true, as I discovered before I'd been back at school for a fortnight. I was lining up in the canteen for my burger and chips when two girls came up behind me.

"Come on, Claire. What are you having?" said one of them.

Her companion hung back.

"Wait a bit," she said.

"What d'you mean? All the tables will be taken—"

"Don't you know who that is? It's Kerry Gilbert. Her brother's that joy-rider who killed little Sophie Jones – you know, they lived next to my gran. Her mum's still in hospital."

"Ugh, no! All right, let's go and sit somewhere else. We don't want to be anywhere near *her*."

Neither of them bothered to lower their voices, and one or two other students gave me curious or scornful looks. I kept my head held high but knew my cheeks were burning. It was so unfair! Mark had been stupid, reckless – but he'd paid for his stupidity with his life. And whatever he'd done, it wasn't my fault.

"Don't take any notice of them. What do they know?" Sue said indignantly when I told her what had happened.

Just when I thought people were forgetting about Mark, the inquest came up, and there were loads more reports in the papers, including interviews with Mrs Jones, who was still in hospital. That meant more stares, more whispers. Some of the local kids paint-sprayed the word KILLER in big letters on our garden wall.

I felt as though my life was falling apart, and there didn't seem anything I could do about it.

The day my best friend Sue told me that her dad had got a new job in Scotland and that they were moving away, I felt like giving up.

"Mum says you can come and stay any time, Kerry," said Sue, who was almost as upset as me. "And I'll write you loads of letters. I promise; and there's always the phone."

"Yes," I said, almost too shocked to speak.

I'll have to leave school – run away or something, I thought desperately. I can't, I just *can't* face all the stares and the looks and the people like that Claire whoever-she-was, without Sue to stand up for me!

"Oh Kerry, I'm sorry," said Sue. She was almost in tears. "I wish this had happened at any other time. I know how you must feel, after Mark dying and everything."

She doesn't know how I feel, I thought bitterly. How can she? No one knows how I feel.

I went home that day ready to tell Mum and Dad that I wanted to leave school altogether or at least transfer to another school where no one knew me, or knew Mark. I'd heard it was possible to do that and it seemed like the answer to all my problems.

As it turned out, I didn't have to.

"Great news, Kerry!" said Dad as I walked through the front door. He had the first real smile I'd seen on his face since the dreadful night when Mark was killed.

"What's that?"

Dad was waving a letter in the air and looking much more like his old self.

"We're moving!"

"What?"

"We're moving to Norfolk."

"Norfolk?" I echoed stupidly.

"Yes. The company is opening a new branch up there and they asked for volunteers to be transferred to the new factory." He cleared his throat. "I thought it would be the best thing for all of us, so I applied. I just heard today that I've been accepted."

At first I couldn't take it in. Norfolk! That was miles away. A new start, a new home, a different school – somewhere no one knew me or knew what had happened. Wasn't that just what I'd been hoping for, praying for? London held too many memories – memories of Mark and the way things had been. Norfolk meant a whole new life for all of us.

I gave Dad a hug.

"Sounds OK to me," I said, feeling more cheerful than I had done for months.

Dad grinned. "That's my girl! See if you can convince your mum, Kerry. She – well, I'm sure she'll come to see it my – *our* way in the end."

I tried, I really did. I could see it was harder for Mum. She'd been more shattered than any of us by Mark's death and by the realization that the son she loved was a car thief. She'd lived in London all her life. She'd miss her friends and my Auntie Cath.

"But you can visit any time, love. There'll always be room for you in our house, you know that," said Auntie Cath kindly.

Mum smiled, but it wasn't a happy smile.

Knowing that I was leaving soon took a huge weight off my shoulders. Even though I was still pointed at in school, and there were a few people, led by Claire Knowles, who turned their noses up at me, I didn't care any more. Just a few more weeks, I thought, and I'll never have to see any of them again.

I was sad when Sue left. We'd been together since primary school and Scotland was a long way away, but knowing that I was leaving too took the edge off even that.

Dad drove us up to Norfolk a couple of times so that we could have a look at the place we'd be living and do some house-hunting.

"How d'you think you'll like living in a small town, Kerry?" Dad asked me. "It'll be a bit of a change from London, won't it?"

I nodded. Yes, I thought, and a change is just what I need. I want to get away from London and all the memories and the pointing, accusing fingers.

It didn't take Mum and Dad long to find us a new house and I liked it at once. It was in a quiet road with a big garden back and front, and it was on the edge of the town so that there were nice heathland walks just moments away.

"It's been perfect for Lulu, here. She'll miss her walkies!" said the lady we were buying from, stroking the fussy little King Charles spaniel which snuffled around our legs.

Perhaps I could have a dog, I thought. I'd always longed for one, but it really wasn't practical in London. Out here, I thought, it'd be perfect.

Oh, I'm going to love it here, I know I am! I thought hopefully. Dad was right. We need to make a new start, the three of us.

I was sorry Mum didn't seem able to see it that way. As we drove back to town, Dad and I chatted excitedly about the house – how he'd decorate my room, which was much bigger than my poky little London bedroom, what he could do in the garden . . . I mentioned the idea of getting a dog, and he seemed quite keen.

But when I looked at Mum, she was slumped in her seat, tears trickling out of the corners of her eyes.

"What is it, love?" Dad said, his voice rough with concern.

Mum shook her head.

"Oh Mum," I said helplessly, "I know it's hard, but it's the best thing, honestly. A clean break."

We made Mum go to the doctor before we left London. She was really kind, but told Dad afterwards that only time would really help. Time, and plenty to think about. Well, I thought, this move will certainly give her that.

Mum didn't take much interest in the actual move. Dad and I did most of the organizing, but neither of us minded. I couldn't exactly say I was happy, but at least I had something to do to take my mind off Mark.

So, when moving day finally came, I was much too busy to feel sad. Sue was up in Scotland and only Auntie Cath and one of our neighbours came out to see us off. No one else bothered.

I don't care, I told myself. I don't have to see any of them again. I'll be living somewhere I can just be me, Kerry Gilbert, not Mark's sister, or the killer's sister, or "that girl whose brother, you know. . ." No one will know what happened that January night.

For the first time since Mark died, I felt free, without a cloud of guilt and shame hanging over me.

I never even looked round as Dad drove us away.

Chapter 2

It was easier once we'd moved.

It wasn't that I didn't miss Mark any more – I did. I thought about him every single day. It was almost as if we'd moved away without him, and left him behind in London, still working on Danny's market stall. I kept half-expecting the phone to ring and Mark to say, "How's it going, Kerry?" the way he used to do.

But I did have other things to think about, and that helped.

It was a bit strange, living in such a small town, after being in London. The first Saturday, I took myself off for a walk.

The centre of town was really pretty in an old-fashioned sort of way. There was a Saturday market, with clothes stalls as well as fruit and veg and farm produce. There was a tiny shopping mall, a café, a McDonald's, a few small shops, a supermarket, the library and the Health Centre and that was it.

I wondered where the young people hung out. I hadn't seen anyone under thirty since I'd arrived, except for a couple of rough-looking bikers coming out of the chippie on the main street.

But there must be *some* young people, I thought. The school I'd be going to after the holidays had about eight hundred students, I'd been told. So where were they all?

I went into McDonald's and ordered myself a milkshake. There were a crowd of girls sitting in one corner who looked about my age, but they didn't take any notice of me. Two guys came in and went over to them, and there must have been some joking and teasing, because the girls all started laughing. I felt a pang of envy. I was determined to settle down and enjoy my new life and it had been a relief to get away from London and all its memories – but at least I'd had friends there. Not many – I was never one of the in-crowd at our school, that's if there was one – but at least I'd had Sue, and Lyn and Tricia.

Then I remembered that Sue was hundreds of miles away in Scotland and I had to blink back the tears. Depression seemed to settle on my shoulders like a black cloud.

Oh God! I thought. Perhaps it's going to be just as bad here as it was at home in London. Perhaps I'll always feel like an outsider. Those girls over there have probably known one another all their

19

lives – they won't want to be friends with me.

I hastily drained the last of my milkshake and hurried out.

As I passed the table of laughing, chattering girls and guys I slipped on a dropped chip and almost fell against one girl.

"Oh! Oh . . . I'm sorry," I stammered, feeling a complete idiot.

A pair of sharp dark-brown eyes looked me up and down and she tossed back a mane of silky black hair.

"S'all right," she said casually. "No harm done."

She turned back to her friends, muttered something in a low tone, and they all burst out laughing.

"You are awful, Val!" one of the other girls said.

My cheeks burned. Were they talking about me?

I'm getting paranoid, I thought, as I left the restaurant and strolled around the clothes stalls, my heart beating fast. Of course those girls weren't talking about me! Why should they be? It wasn't like it had been at home, where everyone knew me and knew what had happened. No one knew me here. I was making a new start.

I could be anything I wanted to be. I could go back into McDonald's right this minute, go up to the girl with the long dark hair and say, "Hi! I'm new in town. Where are the fun places to go round here?"

I could do just that, but I knew I wouldn't.

It was another two weeks before term started at my

new school and I found myself looking forward to it. I had plenty to do, helping Dad with the decorating and the garden, but I had to admit I was pretty bored in the evenings. I was worried about Mum too. She still seemed really depressed, and nothing Dad and I could say or do seemed to cheer her up.

"I've been thinking," Dad said one evening at dinner. "You know, Kerry, you were talking about getting a dog? Would you still like one?"

"Oh *yes*!" I cried. "I'd love one!"

My friend Sue had had a dog, a soppy mutt with floppy ears who'd come from Battersea Dogs' Home. She used to say he was practically her best friend, I remembered.

I was sure I wouldn't feel so lonely if I had a dog and it might cheer Mum up a bit too.

Dad made some enquiries and found out that there was an animal rescue centre in a village about five miles away, run by a local family. When he rang them up, they said yes, they did have some dogs for re-homing and would we like to come and see them?

Even Mum seemed quite excited as we drove off on Saturday morning to the rescue centre. It was down a country lane about a mile out of the village. As soon as we pulled up in the car park I could hear yaps and barks. A tortoiseshell cat with three legs came limping out to greet us.

"That's Toby," said the lady who ran the centre,

a kind-looking person with a weatherbeaten face, wearing jeans and wellies. "He came in after a road accident, needless to say. You wouldn't believe the speed some of the lorries drive through the village!"

"Is he all right?" I said – rather pointlessly, since he obviously was. He wobbled a bit when he walked but seemed to get around OK.

"Oh, yes, he's fine, aren't you, old lad? Now . . . you're the Gilberts, right? You're looking for a dog?"

"That's right," Dad said.

She looked at us searchingly.

"Any particular type?"

"Just – just a family pet. Medium-sized, we thought," said Mum rather shyly.

"Ever had a dog before?"

"No," said Dad. "We've just moved up from London, and now we've got a good-sized garden and some nice walks round about. . ."

"Mmm. Any young children in the house?"

"No."

"Just me," I put in.

"The reason I ask, we're pretty choosy about the homes our animals go to," she said firmly. "We don't want people taking them on a whim, or as a Christmas present for a child who's too young to know what responsible pet ownership is all about. We'll have to have a look at your house, make sure it's suitable."

I felt a bit offended at first but soon realized that

she was right. She couldn't hand out dogs to any old person who came around asking. We might have been going to keep it outside in a cold kennel, for all she knew.

She asked Dad a few more questions and then said, "My daughter will show you the dogs we've got at the moment. Anna? Anna!"

While we waited for Anna to arrive she explained that they had seven dogs ready for re-homing.

"Some strays, some dumped on us, a couple from families where there's been a divorce, one from an old man who died, sadly," she said.

Poor things! I thought. They must wonder what's going to happen to them – if they're ever going to find someone to love them again.

A girl my own age came round the corner of the house. Like her mother she was dressed in jeans and a sweatshirt, with long brown hair tied back, no make-up, and big round glasses. She smiled shyly at us.

"This is my daughter Anna, who helps me out here. She must be about your daughter's age," she said suddenly.

"I'm sixteen," I said.

"So am I," said Anna. "You're not from round here though, are you?"

"Yes, we are – we've just moved in," I said.

"Really? What d'you do? Are you working or—"

"No, I'm still at school," I explained. "I start at

Millbrook Comprehensive after the holidays, in the Sixth Form."

Anna grinned. "Millbrook? That's where I go, too."

Her mother tapped her on the shoulder.

"You'll have to tell . . . er. . ."

"Kerry," I put in.

"Kerry . . . what it's like at your school, but later on, if you don't mind," she reminded her. "They've come to look for a dog. Medium-sized, a family pet. Why don't you show them Jessie? Or Bodger?"

"OK. If you'd like to come this way. . ."

We followed Anna round the side of the house, across the garden and towards some wire-enclosed runs. The first one contained two rather sleepy-looking cats and then we passed a pair of big grey rabbits. As we approached the dogs, there was a chorus of yaps and barks.

"Quiet, Cindy! Skittles! It's only me," Anna scolded gently.

Bodger turned out to be a big black mongrel who sat disconsolately on the grass, worrying at a dog chew.

"He's very friendly," Anna assured us. "And this is Jessie."

I think we all knew – Mum, Dad and me – that Jessie was meant to be our dog, right from the start. She was about the size of a beagle, but with a lot more hair, and two button-like black eyes peering out from under her fringe.

When Anna bent down to her, she "wuffed" a greeting and her ridiculous little stump of a tail began to wag.

"Hello, Jessie girl!" said Anna. "Are you going to come out and make friends?"

She undid the catch and the next thing I knew a cold, friendly black nose was being pressed into my hand.

"Hello, Jessie!" I said softly. "Are you coming home with us, then?"

Jessie wuffed again.

I fondled her soft, floppy ears and she rubbed her head against me.

"Looks like she likes you, Kerry," said Dad. Even Mum was smiling.

"Oh, yes," I said, feeling almost as though I might be going to cry again. It was just the way Jessie's black eyes rested on me, the way she seemed to be begging me to take her home, love her. . .

If I did, I knew she'd love me back, the way dogs do.

I didn't want to make too much of an idiot of myself in front of Anna, so I sniffed hard and said, "She's lovely!" meanwhile letting my hair fall round my face and concentrating on petting Jessie.

When I looked up, Anna was watching me sympathetically. I suddenly had the idea I didn't have to worry, that she knew how I was feeling.

"Looks like love at first sight," she said cheerfully.

"I suppose it is," I laughed.

I wanted to take Jessie home then and there but Anna explained that there were certain formalities to be gone through and that she and her mum would come down in the next day or two to have a look at our house just to make sure it was OK for the dog.

"You do understand, don't you?" she said anxiously. "I'm sure there won't be any problems, but we do have to check."

"I know you do," I said, liking Anna more and more.

When we went back to the house, Anna's mum, Mrs Sheldon, had made a cup of tea.

"Why don't you take Kerry upstairs to your room and tell her a bit about school, while we go through the paperwork?" she suggested.

"Sure," said Anna. "Like a Coke, Kerry?"

She led me up the stairs to a big bedroom, very stylishly decorated with pale furniture and smart striped wallpaper. I looked around enviously. Dad hadn't got round to decorating my bedroom yet, so I was still living with crimson roses which were utterly gross.

"What's it like then, the school?" I asked rather shyly. I was glad I'd met someone who went there; it would make the first day a lot less intimidating.

Anna shrugged. "It's OK. Pretty much like most schools, really. But we do have a brilliant new Sixth-Form block, separate from the rest of the school, so it's all going to be different for all of us this term. I mean, we can make coffee and wear our own clothes and get away from all the screaming brats. I'm looking forward to it."

"It sounds great. Which A levels are you taking?"

"Pure and Applied Maths and Physics. What about you?"

"English and Sociology," I said, disappointed. I liked Anna already and was glad we were going to be at school together. But if she was doing science, we probably wouldn't be able to see much of each other.

"What are the other girls like?"

Was it my imagination, or did she hesitate for a moment?

"Oh, OK," she said. "A mixed bunch, really, like anywhere. There'll probably be one or two new faces this term anyway – besides you, I mean. Some of the other local schools don't have proper Sixth Forms so people tend to end up with us."

That sounded OK too. I wasn't looking forward to being the only newcomer and standing out like a sore thumb.

"It must be hard for you, moving away from all your friends," Anna said sympathetically. "Your dad's got a job out on the new industrial estate, didn't he say?"

"That's right. It's the same firm as he worked for in London and he – well, he fancied a change."

I half-wished I could tell Anna about Mark and just why we had needed to get away. I will, one day, if we stay friends, I promised myself. But not just yet.

Anna was laughing.

"You must find it ever so boring living out here after London," she said.

I'd noticed before that everyone thinks if you live in London you're out in West End clubs every night, mingling with famous people, just like the stories in magazines. It's not like that at all, unless you're rich or you live right in the centre. Sue, Lyn, Tricia and I had only been to a West End club once and then we'd had to leave just when things got going, to catch the last train.

"There's the pictures and a few other places in Norwich, but that's twenty miles away," Anna went on. "It's hopeless if you don't have a car – or a boyfriend with one."

"Have you?" I asked, hoping she wouldn't think I was being nosey.

"No, no chance," she said. "That's something else about living in the sticks, Kerry. Everyone knows everyone and by the time you get to sixteen you've been out with all the fit fellas for miles around."

"Anna? Kerry?" came Mrs Sheldon's voice from downstairs.

We finished our Cokes and went down to where Mum and Dad were waiting.

Mrs Sheldon promised to come round the following evening to have a look at our house and told us that we could collect Jessie the day after that.

28

As we drove home, I felt more cheerful than I had done for weeks – months, even. I'd got a lovely little dog. Dad told me that Jessie was only two years old and had belonged to a couple who were getting a divorce and couldn't keep her. Better still, I had the feeling that I'd found a real friend.

I saw Anna again a couple of times before term started – once when she came round with her mum to have a look at our house, and again when we went to collect Jessie. She told me a bit more about school – that everyone liked the head of the English department, who would probably be teaching me, and that someone new was coming for Sociology. I was really, *really* glad I'd met her. As the first day of the new term drew nearer, I found I was getting quite nervous. I remembered how terrifying the comprehensive had seemed at first, after my little local primary school. But I'd had Sue with me then. This time, I thought, I'd be on my own . . . if it wasn't for Anna.

Jessie was a help, too. It was just like Sue said – a dog can be a real friend when you're feeling a bit down. Jessie settled in with us as if we'd had her all her life. She slept on the end of my bed and when she felt like a walk she'd go and sit by the front door, her head on one side and her tail wagging hopefully. I loved her to bits.

* * *

All the same, I woke up on the first morning of term with butterflies the size of elephants in my stomach. I managed to choke down a cup of tea, but couldn't eat any breakfast. I'd arranged to meet Anna at the school gates – she came in on a bus which went round all the villages – and she said she'd take me to the Sixth-Form block and introduce me to a few people.

The school buildings were pretty impressive, I had to admit. The Sixth-Form block was brand new. There were classrooms, cloakrooms, a small hall, and a common room with a tiny kitchenette and a Coke machine for soft drinks. Anna and I were early and slung our bags down on one of the chairs before sitting down ourselves. If it hadn't been for the smell, I wouldn't have thought I was in school at all. Schools always smell the same though, don't they? A mixture of old dinners, floor polish, and football boots.

Two boys came in and nodded hello to Anna.

"Hi, Simon! Hi, Paul!" she said. "This is Kerry Gilbert, who's joining us this term. She used to live in London."

"Yeah?"

I nodded, feeling suddenly shy.

"What A levels are you doing?"

I told them.

We chatted a bit longer, then they wandered off. Soon afterwards three girls came in and I was introduced again, and told them what my A level subjects were.

"Where are you from?" asked one of them.

"London. My dad's job was transferred up here."

She raised her eyebrows.

"Won't you get bored here, after living in London?"

I sighed as I explained yet again.

More students came and went, then the school secretary, then a tall dark guy with a French accent who, we decided, had to be the new languages assistant. Names and faces went round and round in my head. However will I remember everyone? I thought.

Then, about three minutes before the bell was due to ring for the start of school, I heard the unmistakable thumping beat of heavy bass music. What on earth's that? I thought, puzzled.

The main doors swung open and a group of four or five girls walked in, all talking at the tops of their voices. The girl in front was carrying an enormous ghetto-blaster with the volume turned right up.

Simon, the guy I'd met first of all, turned round with a frown.

"Leave it out, Valerie!" he protested. "Give us a break, why don't you?"

With a shock of surprise, I recognized the girl I'd seen – almost crashed into – in McDonald's that first Saturday. The girl with the long dark hair.

She shrugged.

"Boring!" she said. "This is supposed to be our room, isn't it? I mean, correct me if I'm wrong, but we are supposed to be able to do what we like in here?"

"That doesn't mean we can all play music – if you can call that music – as loudly as we like," bawled Simon, above the din.

Just then a bell rang.

Valerie pouted and turned the music off, much to my relief. I turned to Anna.

"What's that for? I mean, where do we go now?"

"School meeting," she said, "in the main Hall. It's a pep talk by the Head, welcoming us at the start of the new term – that sort of thing."

"I can't wait," said Valerie, obviously over-hearing this. She came over, apparently noticing me for the first time, followed by the girls she'd come in with.

"Hi!" she said confidently, looking from Anna to me and then back to Anna. "Who's this, then? I haven't seen you before – or have I?" She frowned as if she was trying to remember.

"This is Kerry Gilbert. Kerry – Valerie Maxwell," said Anna expressionlessly. "And Judy Priestly, Karen Connor, Amy Flowers and Meg Tate."

More names and faces! I thought desperately. Still, at least I'd remember Valerie Maxwell without any difficulty. For one thing, she was extremely pretty – tall, slim, with the inky-black hair I'd noticed before, dark eyes and a near-perfect complexion. She looked more like a model than a school student.

"Kerry's from London," Anna was saying.

Valerie's eyes narrowed.

"That so? You'll have to tell us country hicks all about it, won't you?"

I wasn't sure whether she was being sarcastic, but she went on eagerly, "Did you ever get to Camden Market? A cousin of mine's got a stall there. I go down quite often. Bit touristy, but it's pretty cool."

"Yes . . . er. . ."

As it happened, I *had* been to Camden Market, but only once. Since we lived in south-east London, it'd taken us about two hours to get there. Valerie probably knew more about it than I did.

"Kerry, we've got to go. The bell's rung," Anna reminded me.

Valerie smiled. "I'll talk to you later," she said firmly, before going off with Karen and Judy and the other girls.

Well, she seems friendly enough, I thought, as Anna and I hurried across the school grounds to the main hall.

"What did you think of Valerie?" Anna panted, just before we reached the Hall.

I shrugged. "Oh, I don't know," I said truthfully. In a way, I was drawn to Valerie Maxwell, but not in the way I'd been drawn to Anna when we first met. She – Valerie – was pretty and stylish and totally confident, in a way that I knew I'd never be. She seemed to be the leader of her little crowd, just as she had been when I saw her in McDonald's. She even seemed to like me, and yet. . .

33

Was I imagining it, or was there something cold about those unfathomable dark eyes – something mocking about her smile?

Don't be daft! I told myself. You've only just met the girl, you're not being fair. You can't go taking an instant dislike to people.

But did I dislike Valerie Maxwell? Or did I just envy her? Or what?

I had plenty of time to decide during my first week at school, because it turned out that Valerie Maxwell was taking the same A level courses as I was. I saw quite a bit more of her than I did of Anna, who did a lot of work in the science labs which were at the other side of the school grounds. I saw Anna at the beginning and end of school, and sometimes when our free periods coincided, but in lessons I spent most of my time with Valerie, Judy, Karen, a little mouse of a girl called Heather who never said anything to anyone, and three guys. That was the English set. Sociology was a bit more mixed, with Simon and Paul, the two boys I'd met on my very first morning, who were quite friendly.

Valerie was the leader of the gang, though. Even the guys seemed to realize it. She and Simon were always having a go at one another, mainly over music. Valerie was a dance music fan, Simon liked indie and metal, and they never stopped arguing about it.

She really stood out from the crowd. The rest of

us had bad hair days, the occasional spot, weight problems. Not Valerie. Judy Priestly always brought salads to school and spent the lunch hours chomping her way through chopped celery and grated carrot and moaning to the rest of us that she hadn't lost even *one* pound. Valerie ate Mars bars and greasy chips from the chippie, smoked – we weren't allowed to smoke in school but that never stopped her – and still looked stunning.

It was the same in class. She'd got A stars for nearly all her GCSEs, never seemed to hand her homework in on time – and got away with it.

Anna had told me Valerie's father was pretty well off, so she always had the best clothes, the latest CDs, her own mobile phone and, according to Anna, the wildest parties too.

"Not that I ever get invited," Anna added.

"Why not?"

Anna hesitated. "You'll probably think I'm bitching, but believe me, Kerry, Valerie Maxwell's only interested in yes-girls," she said.

"Yes-girls?"

"Haven't you noticed? She always hangs round with Judy and Karen and Amy and Meg, and do you know why? Because they think she's wonderful, that's why. She's got an ego the size of Norfolk, that girl."

"You don't like her, then," I said, disappointed. Valerie had been nice enough to me, in a careless sort of way. I could see what all those other girls saw in her.

People who weren't part of Valerie's crowd were outsiders. Like me. And I was sick of being an outsider.

Chapter 3

"Coming down the chippie, Kerry?"

I looked up from my copy of *Henry V.* Miss Latimer, our English teacher, was off with flu and we were supposed to be using this period to study Act III.

"What, now?" I said, surprised.

Valerie laughed. "Why not? There's an hour and a half before the next lesson – plenty of time."

I didn't like to ask her what for. To be honest, I was surprised she'd asked me to join her and the others. She didn't usually bother. We were allowed to go into town in the lunch hour as long as we told a member of staff we were going. I was flattered to be included.

"Oh – OK," I said. "Shall I go and tell Mr Burns or whoever's on duty?"

Valerie raised her eyebrows. "Why? We're big girls, Kerry; we can look after ourselves."

"But I thought. . ."

I felt uneasy about going out without permission. Mr Burns had explained that even though we were Sixth Form, the school was responsible for us and needed to know where we were at all times. It sounded fair enough to me. It was only what Dad and Mum always said.

Trust Valerie not to care about something like that! I thought. I wasn't sure whether I admired her nerve, or thought she was crazy to take the risk. But then, I quite often felt like that about Valerie.

"Well, are you coming or not?" she asked me impatiently.

"I'm coming."

In the end, Karen and Judy and Valerie and I went off together. I'd thought about asking Anna to come with us but I was pretty sure she'd said she was in the Physics lab until lunch-time today. Besides, I knew she wouldn't want to go anywhere with Valerie. She'd made it pretty clear she couldn't stand her.

The chippie was a typical old-fashioned bikers' café, with steamed-up windows, Formica tables, and wheezing old men reading the *Racing Post* at every other table. It smelled of hot fat, cigarette smoke and dirty water.

The guy behind the counter was a balding, middle-aged Italian.

"'Ello, beautiful ladies!" he said, obviously recognizing Valerie and the others. "Finished with school today, have you?"

Valerie grinned. "No, worse luck," she said. "We've got to go back after lunch. What's the special today, Giuseppe?"

"Lasagne and chips," said Giuseppe.

I thought it sounded gross, but when it came it was surprisingly tasty.

We were halfway through our meal when the café door opened and a couple of guys in their mid-twenties, wearing motorbike leathers, came in. One of them raised his eyebrows when he saw us. Valerie ignored him.

After a few moments' conversation with Giuseppe, he swaggered over to us.

"Hi, darlin'!" he said, leaning right over and ruffling Valerie's hair.

She pulled away. "Don't do that," she said icily.

He grinned. "Playing it cool today, are we?" he said.

Valerie didn't reply. Karen and Judy looked down at their plates and didn't say anything either. I wondered what was going on. It sounded as though Valerie and the biker knew one another, but. . .

After a few minutes, he shrugged and went off to join his friend.

"D'you know him?" I muttered to Valerie.

"Pete? He's history," she said coldly.

Oh, well! I thought. It's no business of mine.

By this time the two guys had their heads together. The one who'd spoken kept looking over in Valerie's direction. I felt a bit uncomfortable, and wished we could get away, but Valerie and the others showed no signs of leaving.

We ordered cups of tea and Valerie passed round a packet of cigarettes.

"No, thanks, I don't," I said. I'd already told her several times that I didn't smoke. The others lit up, adding to the fuggy atmosphere and making me feel slightly sick.

"I bet you wish you'd stayed in London, Kerry," Valerie said suddenly. "There's so many great places to go."

"I suppose," I said vaguely. I'd almost given up trying to explain that Wellingham Park, where we'd lived, was just an ordinary outer London suburb and that I hadn't spent my time out clubbing in the West End.

Valerie stubbed out her half-smoked cigarette.

"Fancy going down the pub?" she said casually.

"The pub?" I echoed.

"Val. . ." Karen protested.

"Or don't you drink either?"

Suddenly, her black eyes were mocking me. I had the strangest feeling that I'd been invited out this lunch time as some kind of test.

"Well, I – I do sometimes," I said, truthfully.

"So what *do* you do, Kerry?" Valerie said. "Sex? Drugs? Rock 'n' roll?"

She didn't bother to lower her voice and I could see the bikers looking at us and grinning. I felt really embarrassed, and couldn't think what to say.

"N-not really," I admitted.

"Leave it, Val," said Judy awkwardly. "It's time we were getting back to school anyway."

Valerie shrugged. "S'pose so," she said.

We had to walk past the bikers' table as we left. Pete tried to catch hold of Valerie's arm but she pulled away.

"I'll see you, darlin'!" he said meaningfully.

"In your dreams!" Valerie snapped as she stalked out.

Outside the café Valerie strode off so fast that Judy, Karen and I practically had to run to keep up. She seemed to be in a vile mood. As we walked through the school gates, I caught sight of Anna, coming out of the Physics lab.

"Hi, Anna!" I greeted her.

She smiled at me and made to come over. Then she saw Valerie and the others and her smile faded.

"I'll catch you later," she said, expressionlessly.

Valerie looked scornful. "I don't know why you bother with Anna Sheldon. She's a real geek," she said.

But I wasn't going to let her get away with that. I liked Anna.

"What's wrong with her?" I demanded.

Valerie looked pitying. "Well, if you need me to tell you that. . ." she began. "I mean, look at her! Her clothes, for a start. Her hair. Those geeky glasses. I mean, why doesn't she get herself some contacts?"

"Perhaps she doesn't want to," I retorted hotly.

"Her parents are weird too," Karen put in. "Sort of hippies or something."

"They're not hippies!" I protested. "They run an animal sanctuary out in Tofton St Mary. We got our dog from there; that's how Anna and I met."

"Oh, sorry," said Valerie, not sounding the least bit sorry. "I didn't realize she was such a good friend of yours."

She was smiling in a superior, snotty way that made me feel like slapping her face. Just for a moment, I wondered how I could ever have thought we could be friends, how I could ever have *wanted* to be Valerie Maxwell's friend. Anna was right, I thought angrily. She's only interested in yes-girls, and I'm not one!

Then the bell went for the beginning of afternoon school.

It was hard to keep my mind on nineteenth-century poetry, though. Who does Valerie Maxwell think she is? I thought crossly to myself. Dragging us all off to that awful café, pretending it was such a big deal. . .

I met Anna after school as usual and thought she seemed quiet and sort of subdued. I hoped she wasn't offended that I'd gone off with Valerie and the others. I wouldn't be making *that* mistake again!

Anna was OK the next day, though, and Valerie didn't ask me to go into town with her again, anyway. In fact, she more or less ignored me in school from then on. Not that I cared. I was too busy settling in, trying to remember who everyone was, not to mention getting used to a very different style of working.

Anna was working hard too, but we managed to get together some evenings and at the weekends, so I didn't feel lonely any more.

I'm glad we moved out here, I thought. Dad was right – it made the pain of losing Mark easier to bear.

I'd told Anna about him. I always meant to, and when she came up to my room one evening and saw the photo I kept by my bed, she asked who he was.

"Is that your boyfriend?" she said, pointing.

I laughed, but my heart gave the painful lurch it always gave when I thought about my brother. I shook my head.

"My – my brother Mark," I told her.

"Is he still in London? Away at college?"

I took a deep breath.

"He's – he's dead,' I said.

It still hurt, saying that.

Anna was looking horrified.

"Oh . . . Kerry . . . I'm sorry,' she gasped.

"That's OK. He – he was killed in a car smash last January," I told her. "That was one reason why Dad took the job out here. We wanted to – you know, start again. Make a new life."

Anna squeezed my hand sympathetically.

"Poor you," she said. "It must have been awful for you."

I nodded. "It was."

I hesitated for a moment. Should I tell Anna the rest of the story – that it hadn't been an ordinary car crash? That my brother had died at the wheel of a stolen car and that he'd killed a little girl?

Anna was my friend. She'd understand, I knew she would. But still. . .

In the end I didn't say anything.

As the weeks went by, I began to feel more at home. Anna and I were firm friends, I got on OK with the other kids at school, and with the teachers. Valerie Maxwell made the odd spiteful or bitchy remark to me, or to Anna, but we just ignored her. I got an A for one of my Sociology projects and both Anna and I auditioned for parts in the Sixth-Form end-of-term play. For the first time for months, perhaps years, I decided that I liked school.

And at home, there was Jessie.

Now I knew exactly what my friend Sue had meant when she'd said what a good friend a dog could be. If I was worried about my homework, or about Mum, or about something one of the Maxwell gang had said, I only had to come home and see two bright brown eyes and a furiously-wagging stump of a tail to feel completely cheered up.

"*You* love me, don't you, Jessie girl?" I'd say, as I collected her lead from the peg by the door and set off on a long tramp across the fields at the back of the house. Jessie trotting at my side, stopping to investigate interesting smells in the hedgerows and racing ahead when I threw a stick for her to fetch.

One Saturday afternoon I threw a stick which was half-rotten and it split in half as it flew through the air. While Jessie ran off after one half, the other went flying across the hedge and I heard a sharp "Ouch!" from the other side.

I stopped in my tracks, my heart beating fast. I'd only hit someone!

Oh, no! I thought, horrified. What on earth have I done? Supposing they're seriously hurt? How could I have been such an idiot!

There was a fusillade of barks and Jessie came careering back along the path, closely followed by a black-and-white cocker spaniel. I rounded a bend and there, climbing down from a gate, was a tall young guy in a waxed jacket and jeans, rubbing at a graze on his neck.

I could feel myself going scarlet with embarrassment.

"I – I'm terribly sorry," I faltered. "Did I hit you? I really didn't mean. . ."

He smiled at me.

"Oh, that's OK," he said. "It's only a graze. I was just surprised, that's all. There I was, minding my own business, walking Chippy there, when a blooming great branch falls out of the sky on to my head!"

I peered up at him guiltily, feeling more and

more embarrassed, until I realized he was teasing me.

"I really am sorry," I insisted. "I was just throwing a stick for my dog. I had no idea it was going to split in two like that, honestly."

"Oh, good! I thought for a moment that you didn't like the look of me," he grinned.

Our eyes met, properly for the first time and a shiver went down my spine. Not like the look of him? I thought. Some chance! He was only the fittest guy I'd seen since we'd come to live in the country. Tall, fairish curly hair nicely cut, hazel eyes, a friendly smile. Just my type – if I *have* a type, that is.

And, miracle of miracles, he seemed to like what he was seeing too, judging by the way those hazel eyes lingered on my face and moved down to my figure. I wished I wasn't wearing jeans and a baggy sweater, but at least the jeans were my best Levi's and fitted me really well, and hadn't Anna said my new boots made the best of my long, slim legs?

It seemed the fair-haired guy liked the look of me, anyway, because he didn't make any move to walk away. We just stood there, looking at each other, and smiling in a silly sort of way.

"Do you—?" he started to say.

"Have you—?" I said, at exactly the same moment.

Then we both burst out laughing. Suddenly, I stopped feeling shy and tongue-tied.

"I was going to ask you if you live round here," he said.

"Yes, our house is the last one in Reaper's Close. We moved in about six weeks ago," I told him. "My name's Kerry Gilbert."

"Craig Shaw. I live at Whitegates Farm. And this is Chippy," he added, indicating the spaniel, who seemed to have made friends with Jessie already.

The two dogs trotted on ahead and it seemed quite natural for Craig and me to follow them. When I told him we'd moved from London he was about the first person I'd met who *didn't* say how boring I must be finding it. I was glad about that. Besides, as of about five minutes ago, I thought, things were looking anything but boring round here. Craig Shaw was a hunk by anyone's standards.

"So you're a farmer," I said.

"Me? No," he laughed. "My dad is, and my older brother. I work as a mechanic in the big garage up on the bypass."

"Oh," I said, feeling a tiny bit disappointed. I could just imagine Craig, stripped to the waist and all sun-tanned, forking great bundles of hay around . . . or whatever farmers did (I was a bit hazy on the details).

"How about you?" Craig was asking.

"I'm still at school. I've just started my A level course."

"Yeah? What are you going to do when you leave?"

I shrugged. "College, I suppose. Then . . . I don't know. I haven't really made my mind up."

"I was lucky," he said. "I always knew what I wanted to do. I've loved messing around with engines ever since I was a kid. I was helping Dad drive the tractor from when I was about nine."

We walked on, the dogs running round our feet, chatting easily about school, work, Norfolk, music, movies. . . I decided I'd never met anyone who was as easy to talk to as Craig. No guys, anyway. He had plenty to say for himself, but it wasn't all him – he seemed just as interested in me, and what I thought and felt.

We had lots in common, too. Dogs, of course, and it turned out that we liked the exact same bands, and both enjoyed swimming, and tennis, and detective stories. I told him I'd been on holiday to France last year and he was really envious.

"I've never been abroad at all," he said, "except once, on a day-trip with the school, when I was fourteen."

"How old are you now?" I couldn't resist asking.

"Nineteen."

Three years older than me, I thought. That's just perfect.

I could see the first few houses on the edge of town. In ten minutes, I thought, we'll be at our back gate. That meant Craig had just ten minutes to say something about seeing me again. I hope he does, I thought. I *really* hope he does.

When we got to the gate, I lingered a bit. I didn't

want to make it look obvious, but I didn't want to dash off and leave Craig, either.

"Well," I said, as Jessie scratched at the gate and whined, "it's been nice meeting you. And Chippy."

"Yes," said Craig. "Yes, it has. Perhaps. . ."

"Yes?" I breathed hopefully.

(*Down*, girl! I told myself. There's such a thing as looking *too* keen, you know.)

"Perhaps we could do it again sometime?"

I could feel myself grinning like an idiot.

"Why not?" I managed to stammer. "I try to give Jessie a good long walk every day at the weekends. She – she needs plenty of exercise."

Craig was smiling too. "Oh, so does Chippy," he said solemnly. "Would tomorrow be OK? About three o'clock?"

"Tomorrow would be brilliant," I assured him.

"OK, I'll come and call for you. Bye now," said Craig casually.

He whistled to Chippy, who followed, black ears streaming behind him, as he walked away, leaving me gazing after them.

I flew up the garden path on wings. I just couldn't wait to tell Anna I'd met such a gorgeous guy – and one who seemed interested in me, what was more. But when I rang the Sheldons' number, there was no reply.

I tried calling Anna several more times that night, but the phone just rang and rang. By bedtime, I was beginning to feel worried. Even if she and her parents had gone out, someone should be there to feed the animals.

"Perhaps their phone's out of order," Dad said, when I mentioned it to him. "Why don't you try the operator?"

When I did, I was told there was no fault on the line.

"That's really weird, Dad," I said. "I hope they're all right."

"Don't worry, love. Try again in the morning," he said reassuringly. "Anyway, what's so urgent? You only spoke to Anna this morning, didn't you?"

I nodded.

"Well, then."

Dad was forever going on at me for nattering to Anna on the phone too much, so I thought I'd better drop the subject.

I did try one more time before I went to bed, though. This time I got through, and Mr Sheldon answered the phone.

"It's Kerry," I said, "Is Anna there? She's not in bed, is she? I'm sorry to call so late."

"I'm afraid Anna's in hospital, Kerry," came her father's gentle voice.

"In hospital?" I gasped. "But – but what's happened? Is she all right? What's wrong?"

"Appendicitis," said Mr Sheldon. "She was rushed off to Norwich this afternoon, and they operated this evening."

I remembered Anna complaining of tummy

pains at school. She thought it was just something she'd eaten.

"Oh, poor Anna!" I said. "Is – she will be all right, won't she?"

"Oh, yes, don't worry," said Mr Sheldon. "She'll be fine, Kerry. She'll be feeling a bit sorry for herself for a day or two, but they'll probably let her come home in the middle of the week."

"Is there anything I can do? Can I see her?" I asked anxiously.

"Well, not tomorrow, she'll still be getting over the operation. Perhaps later," said Mr Sheldon. "Or you could wait till she comes home. She'll be off school for a while and I'm sure she'll get bored."

I could hardly take it in, it all seemed so sudden.

"Give her my love anyway, won't you?" I said.

"Of course we will."

I rang off. By that time, Mum and Dad had gone to bed. Jessie whined, and pressed her cold nose into my hand.

Poor Anna! I thought as I went upstairs to my own room, Jessie at my heels. I wonder how long she'll have to be off school?

I'd almost forgotten about Craig Shaw.

Almost . . . but not quite.

He came to the front door to collect me and Jessie the next day. I'd told Mum and Dad that I'd met someone. My parents are pretty cool about that sort of thing. Dad's not the kind to give every guy

I meet the third degree and he and Craig seemed to like one another from the start. Chippy even managed to coax a smile out of Mum. We set off with the dogs in the opposite direction from yesterday. Craig said he'd show me a new walk along the Fen.

"There are water rats along the banks," he told me. "I see them sometimes."

I felt like an ignorant townie as Craig pointed out all kinds of birds and small, scurrying animals I would never have noticed on my own. He could even tell what kind of bird was around from its song.

I was impressed, and said so.

"I'm from London," I said apologetically. "If it's not a budgie or a chicken, I don't know what it is!"

"And you prefer your chickens oven-ready, don't tell me," Craig grinned.

I giggled, liking him more and more.

I told him about Anna's appendicitis and he was really sympathetic.

"Sheldon?" he said, frowning. "Don't they run that animal sanctuary in Tofton St Mary?"

"That's right. Jessie came from there," I told him.

We must have walked for miles, chatting all the time. Oh, he *is* nice! I thought. I *do* like him! When he asked me, halfway through the afternoon, if I'd like to go to the pictures with him in Norwich in the week, I didn't have to think twice. A real date! I thought. I can dress up, instead of wearing jeans and boots, for once. It'll be brilliant.

"Bye, Kerry! I'll pick you up on Wednesday, about seven," he said, as we parted after our walk.

"Craig seems a nice lad," was all Dad said, when Jessie and I came in. "He's a farmer's son, is that right?"

"Yes, only he works as a mechanic. He's been interested in engines ever since he was a little boy," I told him.

"I'm glad you're making friends here, Kerry," said Mum, with one of her sad little smiles. "It can't have been easy for you, leaving London and everything you knew."

"Well, it wouldn't have been the same in London anyway, after Sue moved away," I told her. I'd never said anything to Mum or Dad about the hard time I'd had at school after Mark's death and the inquest and everything. I always thought they had enough to worry about.

"So you're OK here, are you, love?" Dad said anxiously, giving my arm an awkward pat. "You're beginning to settle down?"

I nodded. "'Course I am. I've got Anna, haven't I? And now Craig. Don't worry, everything's going to be fine from now on. You'll see."

I did go and see Anna in hospital, after school on Tuesday. Her parents were going so I went with them. She looked pale and wan, but said she wasn't feeling too bad and promised to show me her scar when she got out.

With her mum and dad around, I didn't really

get the chance to say anything about Craig. I just gave her all the gossip from school – not that there was all that much. She told me that the hospital food was awful but that the surgeon who'd done her op was a dead ringer for George Clooney.

"Honestly, Kerry, I could've sworn it was him when he came round," she giggled. "Ouch! I'm not supposed to laugh; it pulls my stitches."

"You just get better soon," I said sternly, helping myself to a few of her grapes. "School's not the same without you."

Craig arrived at five to seven on Wednesday night. He looked stunning in khaki chinos and a crisp white shirt. I'd changed my mind about ten times when it came to deciding what to wear, and had ended up in the green silk shirt that Anna said exactly matched my eyes, a short black skirt, and high heels.

From the look on his face when I walked into the living room, I could tell he was impressed.

"You look great," he said as he ushered me out to his car. I normally get a bit flustered and embarrassed when anyone compliments me – not that it happens all that often – but this time I managed to smile and say "Thank you" the way you're supposed to.

Just for a moment, I remembered Anna saying that in this town, what every girl needed was a boyfriend with a car.

Perhaps I've found one, I thought, as I examined Craig's clean-cut profile in the darkness. Lucky me. Lucky, *lucky* me!

Chapter 4

The evening went like a dream. It was a good film, Craig treated me to an ice-cream, and when he put his arm round my shoulders, just casually, I tingled all the way down to my toes.

When I turned to face him, and our lips met, there was a strange, hollow feeling in the pit of my stomach, as if I'd gone down too fast in a lift. I'd been kissed before, but never like that. Craig's lips were warm and firm. He tasted of ice-cream and toothpaste, and as his tongue gently explored the inside of my mouth, I practically melted with bliss.

We broke apart, and he smiled at me and brushed my lips lightly with his fingertips.

"I – I really like you, Kerry," he said in a choked voice.

I hugged him tight.

"I like you too," I said truthfully.

He held my hand as we left the cinema and

didn't let go until we reached the car. I climbed into the passenger seat, wishing that he didn't have to take me home, wishing that the evening could last for ever, just wanting to be with him.

"I've been invited to a party on Saturday," he said as we drove out of the city and headed for home. "Would you like to come with me?"

"I'd love to," I told him. "Whose party is it?"

"Oh, a mate of mine at the garage. Steve Stanmore. His parents live in a big house over Thetford way, and they're on holiday. It should be really good."

I was thrilled. Craig wanted to see me again, wanted to take me to a party, wanted me to meet his friends. Just as if we were an item, boyfriend and girlfriend. I looked at his clean-cut profile in the darkness of the car and could hardly believe my luck.

We rounded a corner. As Craig changed gear he leaned over and squeezed my hand without saying anything. My heart missed a beat.

I really, really like him, I thought. In fact, I almost. . .

Was I falling in love? Was this how it felt?

Craig pulled up outside our house and switched the engine off, then turned to face me.

"Kerry, I've really enjoyed tonight," he said, cupping my face in his hands. I trembled at his nearness.

"So – so have I," I murmured. The look in his eyes, so near to mine, was making me feel dizzy.

Then I was in his arms again and it was every bit as wonderful as it had been when he'd kissed me in the cinema – tender, and yet passionate at the same time. When he let me go, I leaned against him, feeling relaxed and comfortable, and yet trembling with excitement, all at once. I could feel his mouth against my hair, his free hand stroking mine. He didn't try anything else, though. I was glad. I'd had enough of guys who thought that taking you out on a date entitled them to a full-scale grope. I was glad Craig wasn't like that, wasn't into rushing things.

After all, we had all the time in the world.

I was late into school the next morning as I had to go to the dentist. I stopped at the card and gift shop on the way to buy a big Get Well card for Anna. I thought I'd ask everyone in the Sixth Form to sign it, to cheer her up. I felt so happy myself, I wanted to spread it around a bit. I had another date with Craig on Saturday, and I couldn't wait to see him again.

Parked outside the back entrance to the school, which was nearest to the Sixth-Form block, I saw a motorbike, with two people standing beside it. I could hear raised voices, and as I drew nearer I saw that one of them was Valerie Maxwell and the other a guy in leathers. He was hanging on to her arm and she seemed to be trying to break away.

"Stop it, Pete!" I heard her say furiously.

It was the guy from the café, the one she had told me was "history". From the look on his face, he didn't see it that way.

"All right, Valerie?" I said as I hurried by.

For once, she actually looked pleased – or was it relieved? – to see me.

"Oh, hi, Kerry!" she said warmly. "Just hang on a minute, won't you? I'm coming."

She wrenched her arm away from Pete's grasp and followed me into the school grounds. She looked flustered and her lips were pressed tightly together.

"Are you OK?" I asked her, as I heard the roar of the bike's engine starting up.

"Men!" she said. "Spend one night with them, and they start to think they own you, don't they?"

I couldn't help feeling rather shocked. Was Valerie saying what I thought she was saying?

"You . . . er . . . he's an ex-boyfriend of yours, then?" I asked.

She shrugged. "Not exactly," she said coolly. "I slept with him, that's all. Once. Big mistake!"

I didn't know what to say. I wouldn't have thought that a scruffy biker was Valerie's type.

"And he wants to see you again?" I hazarded.

"I don't know what he wants, and I don't care," she said impatiently. "He – oh, I wish it hadn't happened, that's all!"

"How did it?"

"I was drunk," she said frankly. "I'd just been – well, I'd just broken up with someone, you know

59

how it is, and I went out looking for a good time, had a few too many, and. . ."

Well, that explains it, I thought, feeling more friendly towards Valerie than I usually did. She seemed so much in control, it was reassuring to know that even she could make a mess of things sometimes.

"Oh, well, he's bound to give up soon, when he realizes you're just not interested," I said comfortingly.

"He'd better," she said grimly. "Anyway, what're you doing being late, Miss Goody-Two-Shoes?"

"Dentist," I said, ignoring the dig. It was just the way Valerie talked. "Oh, and I bought a card to send to Anna. I thought we could all sign it."

She raised her eyebrows.

"Oh, of course," she said, and the sarcastic edge was back in her voice. "Things just aren't the same round here without Anna."

"There's no need to be like that," I said sharply. "You don't have to sign if you don't want to. I just thought—"

"I'll sign, I'll sign, don't worry," she said hastily. "Don't get upset."

We walked over to the Sixth-Form block in an unfriendly silence.

When I told Mum and Dad I was going out with Craig again on Saturday, Dad took out his wallet at once and peeled off a couple of notes.

"Here," he said, handing them to me. "Take yourself into town and buy yourself something new to wear."

"Oh Dad, thanks!" I said, hugging him. A new dress would be a boost to my morale, and if I was going to be meeting Craig's friends I wanted to look my very best. It was a shame that Anna wouldn't be well enough to come with me, but I planned to go round to her place before the end of the week anyway, to let her know what had been going on, maybe even ask her advice about Craig.

"Craig Shaw?" Anna said in an incredulous voice, when I told her what had been happening.

I nodded eagerly. "Yes, that's right. D'you know him, Anna? You must do."

I remembered what she'd said about everyone knowing everyone else in a small town.

"Yes, I know him."

She didn't sound too thrilled and my heart thumped. Oh, no! I thought. Don't say she knows something awful about him, something that's going to put me off. Supposing he's got a girlfriend or something? Even in the starry-eyed state I was in, it had occurred to me now and again to wonder why a hunk like Craig was on his own.

"What is it, Anna?" I faltered. "He's really nice. I mean, he's been really nice to me and we get on ever so well, apart from fancying each other, you know."

"It's not that," said Anna, smiling, though she

61

still looked troubled. "It's just – did he tell you that he used to go out with Valerie Maxwell?"

Suddenly, the warm autumn evening seemed colder.

"N-no," I admitted. "He didn't. Why should he?"

I thought back to the long conversations Craig and I had had, out walking the dogs. We hadn't really talked much about ex-girlfriends, or ex-boyfriends – not that there was much to tell in my case. Craig certainly hadn't mentioned Valerie, though he must have known I knew her.

Still, I thought, perhaps they hadn't gone out together long. Valerie didn't exactly strike me as a one-man girl; in fact, everything she'd ever said and done suggested exactly the opposite. And hadn't Anna said that everyone round here had dated pretty much everyone else round here by the time they were sixteen, anyway? Craig was bound to be someone's ex.

It still gave me a chilly feeling inside to think of him being Valerie's, though.

"Oh, well," said Anna shrugging, "they broke up some time ago – at least I think they did. I used to see them around town together but that was back in the spring."

"Who cares, anyway?" I said, sounding more confident than I felt. "Craig and I really hit it off, Anna. We like all the same things, he kisses like a dream, and even our dogs like each other!"

Anna giggled. "Well, go for it, Kerry!" she said.

"I always thought Craig was a nice guy. Much too good for that cat Valerie."

I told her about meeting Valerie with Pete the biker, outside school.

"She's going to get herself into real trouble one day," said Anna darkly. "Blokes like that don't take kindly to being messed about."

"It's funny she hasn't got a boyfriend," I mused. "I mean, I know you don't like her, and I don't much myself, come to that, but she's great-looking, you've got to admit."

Anna sniffed. "She *was* supposed to be seeing Mick Greenyer, whose dad owns the *County Press*," she said. "I don't know if she still is."

"That figures," I replied. I could imagine Valerie with some newspaper magnate's son. I couldn't imagine her with Craig. Not that I wanted to!

"Well, never mind about her," I said impatiently. "Dad's given me forty pounds to go shopping for clothes on Saturday, before the party. What d'you think I ought to get?"

"You're asking *me*?" Anna hooted, sounding much more like herself. "I haven't a clue about fashion, you know I haven't."

"Maybe, but you know what colours go with what, don't you? Craig really liked me in that green silk shirt. D'you think I should go for a sophisticated look, or drop-dead sexy, or something more casual? What sort of things do people wear to parties out here?"

We spent an hour discussing clothes and parties

and I went home feeling quite a bit happier. So Craig is an ex of Valerie's, I thought. Well, so what? He's made it pretty clear he's happy to be with me for now.

And for the future, I hoped.

I spent about two hours traipsing round the shops on Saturday looking for exactly the right outfit. There were plenty of slinky black dresses but I thought they might make me look too old. On the other hand, pink and pale blue were too school-girlish, I decided. Being blonde – well, fairish – it was important not to look too washed out. Maybe I should treat myself to some new make-up too.

I was almost ready to give up and settle for the velvet-jeans-and-pretty-top that had been my old standby for London parties, when I saw the dress in a shop window. It was a slip dress in pale jade-green, very simply made – the sort of dress that would look amazing on someone with a slim figure and long legs and matching green eyes.

Me, in fact. It might've been made for me.

Even the shop assistant said "Wow!" when she saw me in it.

It cost a bit more than the forty pounds Dad had given me, but I didn't mind digging into my savings for once. After all, it was a special occasion.

It took me hours to get ready on Saturday night but when I saw Craig's face and heard him say "Kerry, you look stunning!" I felt it had been worth the trouble. My silver party sandals looked just right with the dress. I couldn't walk far in them and they pinched my toes terribly but, I reasoned, you had to suffer to be beautiful. And the way Craig was looking at me made me *feel* beautiful. I just knew it was going to be a fantastic party.

It was about ten miles to Steve Stanmore's place. It turned out to be a big old Victorian house in the country, with lights blazing from every window and a sound system you could hear from the main road. Steve had really gone to a lot of trouble, stringing Christmas-tree lights in the grounds and clearing all the furniture out of a big downstairs room so that we could dance. He and his girl-friend, Julie, were so friendly and welcoming I didn't feel like a stranger for long.

"Come and dump your coat upstairs," Julie chattered as the guys began a conversation about cars. "It's lovely to meet you, Kerry. Have you known Craig long?"

"No," I admitted, as I combed my hair and applied some more lippy. "I only met him last week but I feel as though I've known him all my life. We just hit it off from the start."

"According to Steve, Craig hasn't stopped talking about you all week," Julie said. "He was really curious to meet you. He said he hadn't known Craig as smitten with anyone for ages."

I sat down suddenly among the coats. It was all almost too much for me.

"I hope he's right," I said fervently.

"Come down and have a drink and meet some people," Julie said.

Everyone was really friendly. I met Julie's sister and her boyfriend, a guy who worked at the garage with Craig, two girls from Norwich called Wanda and Marie, a Tim, two Daves, and a guy whose name I didn't catch who told me a joke about a Scotsman and a crocodile that went on and on and on.

"Come on, Kerry, let's have a dance," said Craig, taking my hand and pulling me into the room where the sound system was pounding out dance music. I danced with him and with Steve and then with Craig again. When the music changed to a slow, dreamy number I rested my hot cheek against his shirt and wondered how it was possible to feel so happy.

Everything has worked out just fine, I thought. Dad was right. We needed to make a new start, meet new people, make new friends. Only I never could have dreamed I'd meet someone like Craig.

I looked up at him longingly and he bent his head and kissed me. I could feel the warmth of his body through his shirt.

"Craig?" I murmured dreamily.

"Mmmm?"

"Thanks for bringing me tonight. I'm having a wonderful time."

He smiled and held me tighter.

"Me, too."

What was it Julie had said? Craig was smitten? Well, I was smitten, too, I decided.

"Would you like another drink, Kerry?" Craig asked.

"I wouldn't mind."

Arms round each other, we made our way towards the dining-room, where there was a buffet at one end and the bar at the other. Craig was just pouring out two glasses of wine when I heard a familiar voice from the doorway.

"Well! Fancy meeting you here!"

I looked round, and there, framed in the doorway, stood Valerie Maxwell. She was wearing the shortest, tightest black dress I'd ever seen, her hair spilling over her shoulders in an ebony cloud.

"Hello, Valerie," I said.

She gave me a look of pure hatred, and said nothing. Instead, she sidled across the room and put her hand on Craig's arm.

"Hello, Craig," she purred.

His face was quite expressionless.

"Hello," he said, and went on pouring the wine.

There was an awkward silence. There were one or two other people in the room, including Marie and Wanda, the two girls I'd met earlier, who scuttled out almost at once, exchanging glances. One of the Daves was there too, and he raised his eyebrows at Craig.

"Would you like a drink?" he said politely to Valerie.

"It's all right. Craig will get me one, thanks," she said icily.

What is all this? I thought. I wished I'd had the chance to ask Craig more about his relationship with Valerie – how long they'd been together, when they'd broken up, and on what terms. It looked as though they hadn't exactly parted friends. Still, I thought, he's with me now.

Craig poured another glass of wine and handed it to Valerie without a word. A tall, thin guy with sandy fair hair and an expensive-looking jacket had come in just behind her.

"Oh, there you are. I've been looking for you," he said fussily.

Valerie barely glanced at him; she was too busy watching Craig. After a few seconds, I came to life. I wasn't just going to stand there and watch Valerie Maxwell ogle my boyfriend, for God's sake! And he *was* my boyfriend now, whatever he might have been in the past.

"Come on, Craig," I said calmly. "Let's go and find Steve and Julie."

But as we went out of the room with our drinks I could feel that my hands were shaking.

Craig was looking sheepish. "Sorry about that," he said, when we arrived in the other room. "Valerie's an ex-girlfriend of mine. I had no idea she would turn up tonight."

"I know," I said.

He looked puzzled. "What d'you mean, you know?"

68

I told him that Anna had already told me he and Valerie had been out together.

"That's the trouble with living in a small town," he said, running his fingers through his fair hair in frustration. "Everyone knows everyone else. If you're seeing someone or you break up, the whole town knows about it practically before you do."

I laughed. "Never mind," I said. "I take it you and Valerie didn't exactly end up as good friends?"

He pulled a face. "How did you guess? She's trouble, that girl. I should've known it from the start. One or two people did warn me but I – well, I suppose it was the old male pride thing. I thought I could handle it, or rather her."

"And you found out you couldn't?"

He gave a bitter little laugh. "It was more that I didn't want to, to be honest," he said. "We went out together for about three months – if you can call it going out. All we ever seemed to do was fight. She's a real drama queen you know. Never happy unless she's causing trouble."

"Tell me about it!" I said ruefully. I knew what Valerie was like well enough, after being in the same class as her for nearly two months. Clever, witty, fascinating – she could be all those things, but she was also bitchy and sarky and loved being the centre of attention.

"Anyway, I knew it'd never work out," Craig went on. "I know there are guys who go for women like that, like to show them who's boss and all that, but I'm not into it. So I told her it was all over."

"*You* told *her*?" I echoed. Somehow, it was hard to imagine Valerie Maxwell getting dumped, even by Craig. Knowing her as well as I did, I was sure she wouldn't have been able to cope with the blow to her ego.

Craig nodded. "I was glad to see the back of her and her tantrums," he said.

I swallowed hard. "Did – did you dump her for someone else?" I asked.

He shook his head. "No. And I haven't taken anyone else out since," he said. "Not till I met you."

"Honestly?"

"Honestly."

Craig caught my hands in his. "That's the truth, Kerry, really it is. After Valerie, I decided I'd give women a rest for a bit. It seemed too much like hard work if they were all like her. But then I met you, and you were. . ."

"I was. . ." I prompted, leaning against him. His arm tightened round me.

"Well . . . the exact opposite. Normal and friendly. Someone I could talk to, share things with – not someone who played silly games with me. You and me – that's the way it should be, I reckon. Don't you?"

It was the nicest compliment I'd ever been paid.

"Oh, yes, Craig," I said. "That's just how I feel."

As Craig kissed me all my doubts and fears seemed to fall away. Just for a moment, seeing

Valerie looking so glamorous and so sure of herself, I'd experienced a pang of fear. Suppose Craig wanted her back?

But now that he'd explained that he had been the one to finish things, I knew that wasn't going to happen. He'd already made it more than clear that it was me he wanted to be with, not Valerie. Anyway, she seemed to be with the fair bloke who'd followed her into the dining-room. She obviously just had it in for Craig for dumping her all those months ago.

Typical Valerie, I thought. She has to be the world's worst loser.

"Let's forget about her, OK? Don't let her ruin our night," I pleaded.

Craig looked as though he was going to say something else, but then he smiled and shrugged and we went back to the music.

We danced for a bit longer and then Steve and Craig got involved in another discussion about cars. I looked around for Julie but she seemed to have disappeared, so I wandered back into the dining-room and helped myself to a couple of sausages on sticks. There was no one else around as I stood there, munching. I heard the tap-tap of heels coming along the hallway, then Valerie walked into the room and closed the door behind her.

"Hello again," I said warily. I had no intention of picking a fight with her.

"I didn't know you were seeing Craig Shaw," she said coldly.

I just stopped myself from snapping that there was no reason why I should tell her. What business was it of hers, anyway?

"I am," I said. "We met out walking our dogs."

Valerie's lip curled. "How sweet!" she said.

I shrugged and turned away. The next minute she was beside me, her hand gripping my arm. I was so startled I nearly dropped the glass of wine I was holding.

"I used to go out with him," she said.

"Yes, I know you did."

There was a moment's silence. I could hear her breathing fast.

"I want him back, Kerry," she said simply.

I just looked at her. Part of me wanted to laugh, she looked so intense. If it had been anyone else, I probably *would* have laughed, and said something like, "Well, tough! He's with me now." But there was something in Valerie's dark eyes that stopped me. Something that didn't seem funny at all.

"I'm sorry," I said gently. "Craig told me that — that things just didn't work out between you. Aren't you with . . . er. . .?"

Valerie laughed scornfully. "Mick?" she said. "He's OK – loads of dosh and a fancy car, anyway. But it's Craig I really want."

You spoilt bitch! I thought angrily. You really think you only have to snap your fingers and any man will come running, don't you? Well, not this time. Craig doesn't want you, he wants me!

I tried one more time. "Don't you understand, Valerie? It's all over."

She shook her head, smiling. "I'm afraid *you're* the one who doesn't understand," she said calmly. "I want Craig Shaw back. What's more, I intend to get him!"

Chapter 5

I stared at Valerie without speaking. What a nerve! I thought. How dare she! Craig had already made it perfectly clear to me – and to her – that he wasn't interested in going out with her again. How dare she think she only had to snap her fingers and he'd change his mind!

Anyway, what about me? I was Craig's girlfriend now. I wasn't just going to sit there like a dummy and let her walk off with my guy, was I? I might be shy and quiet, and not the superstar of the Sixth Form like Valerie, but I wasn't a total wimp, either!

"Isn't that up to Craig?" I said icily. "He doesn't want you any more, Valerie. He told me you were more trouble than you were worth."

Valerie's confident smile didn't waver. She gave a short laugh. "Men don't know what they want," she said. "I'll get him back, Kerry. You'll see."

For the first time ever, I knew how people feel

when they get into fights. I was so mad I could've scratched Valerie's eyes out, clawed at her perfect olive skin until the blood ran. Anything to wipe that smug grin off her face.

"No, you won't," I said through clenched teeth. "You'd better just leave him alone!"

"Or what?" Valerie sneered.

Our eyes met and I could see the mockery in hers. I was determined to stare her out, not to be the one to look away. I didn't want to pick a fight with Valerie Maxwell, but if she thought I was just going to give up Craig because she wanted me to, she could think again. Craig was the best thing that'd happened to me in months. He was worth fighting for.

"Or you'll be sorry," I said simply.

To my horror, Valerie burst out laughing.

"I don't think so," she said insolently. "I think you'll find that round here, what I want, I get. You're the one who's going to be sorry."

I felt a chill of fear, but I was determined to stand my ground.

"We'll have to see about that, won't we?" I said, trying to ignore the way my heart was pounding. After all, what could Valerie actually do? It might make her mad that Craig and I were together but I was pretty sure that whatever she did, he wouldn't go back to her.

The door opened and Steve, Julie and a couple of other people burst into the room, talking and laughing.

"What's going on here?" Steve said, looking from me to Valerie and back to me again and raising his eyebrows.

"N-nothing. We were just talking," I said.

At the back of the group I could see Mick, the guy Valerie had come with, peering anxiously into the room.

"Oh look, Valerie, there's Mick," I said sweetly. "Weren't you looking for him?"

She gave me a filthy look and turned away.

I went back into the living-room and found Craig still talking to some of the other guys. As soon as he saw me he slipped his arm round my shoulders and I felt reassured. It's going to be fine, I thought. We're not going to let a bitchy ex of Craig's come between us.

"All right, Kerry?" he said. "Are you having a good time?"

I hesitated and then nodded.

Craig frowned. "You don't sound all that sure."

I might have known, I thought. I couldn't pretend with Craig. Not that I really wanted to. I'd have to tell him.

I pulled him away from the others and along the hall into a quiet alcove away from the pounding beat of the DJ's sound system.

"Kerry, what on earth's the matter?" he said.

I tried to smile. "Oh, I've just had a bit of a ruck with Valerie Maxwell," I said, trying to sound casual.

"What about?" said Craig, sounding puzzled.

"You."

"Me? What d'you mean?"

"She was warning me off," I said. "She said you didn't know what you really wanted."

Craig was still looking totally bewildered.

"And what you really wanted was her, not me."

To my astonishment, Craig burst out laughing.

"What?" he said incredulously. "She's got to be kidding, Kerry! I told you how it was when we were together, didn't I? I wouldn't go out with Valerie Maxwell again if she was the last woman on earth and that's the honest truth."

"Sssh! Keep your voice down," I begged, looking around in case Valerie was anywhere near. I was glad to hear Craig say it, but. . .

"You weren't worried about it, were you?" Craig went on, giving my hand a loving little squeeze. "I promise, you haven't a thing to worry about, Kerry. I'm with you now – and believe me, I know exactly what I want."

The expression in his eyes made me feel funny inside. He *does* care, I thought.

And it *is* all over with Valerie, just like I said. She'd just have to accept that.

But would she?

Craig and I went back into the living-room and had a couple more dances and a chat with Steve and Julie. There was no sign of Valerie or Mick, the guy she'd come with. Perhaps they've gone, I thought, relieved. After what Craig had said,

I should've felt totally reassured. Only somehow, I didn't. I kept remembering Valerie's angry face, the way she'd gripped my arm, her arrogance. She wouldn't give up easily, I knew that.

Suddenly, I remembered her telling me how she'd got involved with Pete the biker. She'd got drunk, she said, after breaking up with someone. Did she mean Craig? Was he the "someone" she'd broken up with? I would probably never know.

I sighed, and moved closer to Craig. At least we're on the same side, I thought. And he doesn't want Valerie back.

It was about ten minutes later that I saw her come in, stalk over to the DJ and say something to him. We were just talking by then and there were about three or four couples on the dance floor. I watched Valerie out of the corner of my eye. Perhaps she's asking the DJ to play her favourite track, I thought to myself uneasily. Then the music stopped and the DJ said that he'd had a request. A few moments later a song I didn't recognize – sort of Spanish-sounding, but with a heavy beat – blared out from the speakers. It wasn't a bit like the sort of tracks that had been playing all night – we'd had some house music, some drum 'n' bass and some Seventies-style disco. All music you could dance to.

This was different. One of the couples walked off the floor straight away, the other two tried their best to move to the beat and eventually gave it up as a bad job. Which just left Valerie.

Alone on the dance floor, her long, dark hair loose and swirling about her, her short dress flaring out with the music, exposing rather a lot of long, slim thigh, her body moved sinuously in time to the music. People were watching, turning, staring. The guy who'd told me the joke earlier was gazing as if he couldn't take his eyes off her and most of the other guys looked pretty gobsmacked as she shimmied and twisted and stamped her feet like some sort of gypsy dancer.

"Fancies herself, doesn't she?" down-to-earth Julie whispered in my ear. Like most of the girls — and me — she thought Valerie was just showing off.

It was different for the fellas, though. They looked all dopey and mesmerized, as if they'd never seen anyone dance before. By the time the track had finished, a small, admiring circle of about six guys were standing there, watching.

I was glad to realize that Craig wasn't among them. He'd seen what Valerie was doing, of course, but then he'd just raised one eyebrow and carried on talking to the rest of us.

That wasn't good enough for Valerie, obviously. She tossed back her hair with a theatrical gesture and came over to where we were standing, pushing past poor Mick as if he didn't exist.

"Dance with me, Craig," she said, totally ignoring me and everyone else.

Stupid cow! I thought. I mustn't let her get to me: she's only trying to wind me up after what we said in the dining-room. She wasn't just asking Craig to dance – it sounded more like she was ordering him to.

When all he said was "No, thanks," very calmly and evenly, I felt like cheering.

Valerie pouted. "Oh, come on!" she said, seizing his hand and trying to drag him on to the dance floor.

He shook her hand away as if it was a wasp bothering him.

"No, thanks, Valerie," he repeated. "I'm not dancing just now."

Julie and I exchanged glances. I must admit, I was trying very hard not to smile. That just serves you right, Valerie Maxwell! I thought.

Valerie shrugged. "Be like that, then," she said coolly, and strode away. As she did so, her eyes met mine, and I was shocked at the expression in them.

It was hatred. Pure, venomous hatred.

It made me shiver.

"Who is that girl?" Julie was asking. "I don't think I know her."

"Valerie Maxwell," I said briefly. "She's in the Sixth Form with me. We do some of the same courses."

"Is she weird, or what?" Julie asked. "I mean, all that flinging herself around on the dance floor with her knickers showing – what was all that about? Didn't she come with Mick Greenyer? He's a nice guy: what was he supposed to think?"

I couldn't help giggling. Valerie had been trying so hard to look sexy and sensuous, and to hear matter-of-fact Julie describing her that way was a scream.

"She's an ex of Craig's," I told her.

Julie's eyes widened. "Is she?"

"Extremely ex," Craig put in. "She always was a drama queen; that's really why I packed her in. She can't stand not being the centre of attention all the time. It was a real pain."

"I bet it was," said Julie sympathetically. "Hey, I'm going to ask the DJ to put some decent music on. Anyone coming?"

I didn't notice what happened to Valerie or Mick after that. She must have persuaded him to take her home, because when Craig and I left there was no sign of Mick's sports car in the drive.

Craig parked outside our house and turned to me.

"I hope Valerie didn't spoil the evening for you, Kerry," he said anxiously. "I've really enjoyed being with you."

"Oh, so have I," I told him. "It was a brilliant party – and I really liked Steve and Julie."

"Good. I'm glad."

Our faces were centimetres apart. He's beautiful, I thought. He's so beautiful . . . and he wants to be with me. I'm so lucky!

Craig's kiss sent shivers down my spine. I felt as if my whole body was melting with tenderness and love as his arms tightened round me. It was like coming home. We're meant to be together, I thought dreamily, as he ran his warm fingertips lightly across my lips.

"Let's meet in the week – go out for a drink or something," he murmured against my hair. "Which nights are you free?"

I just stopped myself from blurting out that I was free whenever he wanted me. It wasn't quite true. I'd agreed to go over to Anna's to tell her about the party and I had a sociology project to hand in at the end of the week.

"Maybe Tuesday? Or Wednesday?" I suggested.

"OK," Craig said, giving me a final hug. "I'll call you. Thanks for a great evening."

"Typical Valerie Maxwell!" Anna snorted, when I told her what had happened. "She probably never even thought about getting Craig back until she saw him with you."

"He's not interested, anyway," I told her. "He told me he wouldn't go back with her if they were marooned on a desert island together – or words to that effect. All the same, Anna. . ."

I hesitated.

"What?"

I wasn't sure how to explain. My common sense told me that there wasn't much Valerie could do. She couldn't *make* Craig go back with her if he didn't want to. Yet I couldn't forget the sheer malevolent hatred in her eyes when she'd looked at me. I got the feeling that if there was anything she could do to hurt me, or put me down, she'd do it without a second thought.

"I don't know," I said slowly. "I get the feeling it's not the greatest idea to get on the wrong side of Valerie. She strikes me as a pretty bad loser."

"She's not any kind of loser," Anna sniffed. "Valerie's used to winning, that's the trouble. She probably can't face the idea that Craig dumped her in the first place, never mind the fact that he prefers you."

"Oh, that's it, cheer me up," I groaned. "What d'you think she'll do? Poison my burger in the school canteen?"

"You wouldn't be able to tell the difference anyway," giggled Anna. "Those burgers are vile."

Anna and I went on chatting about the party and Craig and everything else but I couldn't help feeling uneasy. I wanted to make friends, at school and in town. Not enemies – and certainly not enemies like Valerie Maxwell.

Going to school on Monday, I actually felt quite nervous again. Anna still wasn't back, so I didn't even have anyone to go in with. Luckily, I met Paul and Simon just outside the Sixth-Form block so in the end I went in with them.

"Good weekend?" Simon asked me. "Go anywhere nice?"

"My boyfriend took me to a party near Thetford," I said. I quite liked the idea of calling

Craig "my boyfriend". It seemed a bit cheeky but then, that was what he was, wasn't it? My boyfriend – the first real boyfriend I'd ever had. And there was no way I was going to let Valerie Maxwell spoil that.

Valerie more or less ignored me for most of that day, but then she often did, so that was nothing new. I sat with Heather and Simon and a couple of the other guys from sociology at lunch-time. Valerie seemed to have disappeared and so had Judy and the rest of their crowd. Probably bunked off to the chippie, I decided, breathing a sigh of relief.

Maybe Valerie had seen sense, in the cold light of day. Maybe she'd realized that Craig had meant what he said. Maybe everything was going to be OK. . .

Or so I thought, until I got back from a lesson and found that a file full of notes I'd made for my sociology project was spread all over the floor. It looked as if someone had spilled coffee on them too, including some diagrams I'd painstakingly drawn on my home computer, which were ruined.

"Oh, no!" I wailed, gathering up the scattered sheets of file paper. "Look what's happened. I could've sworn I left those in my locker. How did they get there? They're ruined. I'll have to do the diagrams again."

"Maybe they blew off the shelf. Look, the window's open," suggested shy Heather.

"Mmm. Maybe," I said, looking through them. Was there anything I could salvage or would I have to write everything out again? That would take ages, and I was supposed to be going out with Craig in the week.

I looked up and saw Judy Priestly and Karen Connor exchanging glances. Over the other side of the room, Amy Flowers was grinning. There was no sign of Valerie, but I couldn't help wondering if she and her cronies had had anything to do with this. I could've sworn I'd shut those papers up, and I wasn't usually careless.

"What a shame!" cooed Meg Tate as if in sympathy. "All that hard work wasted!" She was looking really, really innocent – or trying to, anyway.

"I suppose you don't know anything – how it could have happened, I mean?" I demanded bluntly.

Meg's blue eyes widened.

"Me? Not a thing," she assured me.

I didn't believe her.

I mopped the coffee-stained pages hopefully but I could see that at least half my work would have to be done again. I bet that lot had something to do with it, I thought angrily – even though I can't prove anything.

The next day, someone jogged my arm in the canteen as I was carrying a tray, and a helping of baked beans slid off the plate and spilled all down my dress. This time I was even more certain it was no accident. The plate broke, crockery and cutlery flew everywhere, and one of the catering staff rushed up with a J-cloth and a bucket. Again, there was no sign of Valerie, but Judy and Karen were sitting at a nearby table, tittering behind their hands. They were pathetic, I decided. If that was their idea of a joke. . .

"Are you sure it was them?" Craig asked me. I'd told him I could only meet him for a very quick drink as I'd have to re-write half my sociology project before the end of the week. It was worth it though. My spirits rose as soon as I saw him sitting waiting for me.

I shrugged. "Pretty sure. Who else would do that kind of thing? Course, I can't prove anything."

Craig took a long drink from his pint.

"God, girls can be bitches!" he said angrily. "Blokes just thump each other and forget it. Girls go on and on getting at each other."

I smiled at him. "Don't worry," I said. "I'm not going to let them get to me."

He took my hand in his.

"You will tell me if anything else happens, won't you?" he said anxiously. "I – I feel sort of responsible. I mean, I did go out with Valerie. . ."

"It's not your fault, Craig," I said. "It's just the way Valerie is. She doesn't like losing."

He leaned over the pub table and gave me a long, lingering kiss. A crowd of guys playing darts nearby whooped and cheered and I could feel myself blushing. I didn't really mind, though. Craig seemed to be trying his best to let me and the whole world see that it was *me* he wanted to be with.

And I wasn't about to argue with that.

Anna was due back at school the following Monday. I was looking forward to it. At least when she was there I felt there was someone on my side. She had no time for Valerie and didn't mind showing it.

For the rest of the week there were no more practical jokes, and if Valerie and her gang didn't exactly make me feel like their favourite person, they didn't do anything else either. As far as they were concerned, I seemed to have become invisible. Not that I cared. I was quite happy to go round with Simon and Paul in lesson time, and Anna when she came back.

I went to the market on Saturday and the first person I saw in the market square was Simon. Paul was a few steps behind him – those two never seemed to go anywhere without each other – and they were looking at CDs on one of the stalls. We chatted for a bit and then they went off together. I watched them, idly: one tall and fair and chatty, one short and dark and silent. They reminded me of Wallace and Gromit. I giggled to myself, and then some trainers on another of the stalls caught my eye and I forgot about them.

That night Craig took me clubbing in Norwich and we had a fantastic time. Even though we didn't get home till almost three in the morning, we were still up and about on Sunday in time to take

Jessie and Chippy for a long country walk. That was one of the great things about Craig, I decided: he was just as much fun whatever we were doing – going clubbing or to a party, or tramping through muddy fields throwing sticks for our dogs. There really wasn't anything I did that wasn't more fun now that I had Craig to do it with.

It must be love, I decided. When I was with him, I could push the Valerie Maxwell problem right to the back of my mind. Well, almost.

Anna came back to school on Monday, as planned. She still looked a bit pale and wan and she wasn't going to be able to do any gym or games for a while, but she said she felt OK. I'd told her about the weird things that'd been happening. She thought it probably was Valerie and her gang, but advised me to ignore them.

"They'll soon get fed up if you don't let them see they're winding you up," she said comfortingly.

I hoped it was true.

"How was your weekend?" Anna asked me.

"Great!" I said. "Craig and I took the dogs out yesterday, and on Saturday night we went out clubbing in Norwich. On Saturday afternoon . . . let me see. Oh, yes, I went round the market and bought a couple of CDs. I ran into Simon and Paul."

I lowered my voice. "Do those two remind you of anyone?" I murmured.

Anna looked puzzled.

"I don't think so. What d'you mean?"

I started to laugh. Honestly, I didn't mean to be

nasty, it was just a light-hearted comment to make Anna smile.

"Wallace and Gromit!" I hissed.

Anna grinned and looked over to the other side of the room, where Simon and Paul, heads close together, were reading one of the papers.

"I don't think I've ever seen Simon without Paul, or Paul without Simon," I added casually, as we walked over towards the door, past Valerie, Meg, Judy and a couple of the others who were standing just in front of Simon and Paul.

Valerie promptly turned round and gave me the most peculiar look. How can I describe it? Surprised? Malicious? Pleased with herself? It was all of those. And more . . . But I'd given up trying to work out what went on in Valerie's devious little mind, and as I said goodbye to Anna and headed for my English class, I forgot about her.

I was on my way home that evening when I heard hurrying footsteps behind me and turned round to see Simon, sports bag in hand, with Paul three steps behind, as usual. Anna had already gone to get her bus and I was glad to have someone to walk part of the way home with so I called, "Hi, you two!"

To my utter amazement, Simon totally ignored me – just strode straight past with his nose in the air as if I didn't exist.

I couldn't believe it.

"Simon?" I said, bewildered. "Paul? What's wrong?"

"I hope you're satisfied!" Paul hissed as he almost ran to catch up with his friend.

"But . . . what on earth's going on?" I called after them. Neither of them turned round.

"Paul? Simon?"

Silence.

I carried on walking towards the school gates, my mind in a whirl. Whatever had happened? Both guys had looked really upset – angry, even. But why? I hadn't seen them since lunch time and they'd been perfectly OK then.

I racked my brains. Then an idea occurred to me. Perhaps someone – OK, perhaps Valerie or one of her cronies – had overheard me calling them Wallace and Gromit.

No, I decided, it couldn't be that. Even if they had heard, it was a harmless joke – nothing to get into a state about, surely?

I thought about the guys' odd behaviour all evening, but I couldn't come up with any explanation. Not one that made any sense, anyway. I decided that I'd talk to them first thing the next morning, find out what had made them so mad.

"Gay?" I gasped, almost too shocked to speak. "But I didn't – I never – I wouldn't—"

"That's not what we heard," said Simon stonily, his blue eyes unfriendly. Paul shuffled his feet and looked horribly embarrassed. As well he might. According to Simon, I'd been spreading rumours that he and Paul were gay.

I thought, frantically, if there was *anything* I'd said that could have been taken that way. The idea had truly never even entered my head – and if it had, I wasn't the kind to spread rumours. I knew how that sort of thing could hurt, didn't I?

"Simon," I faltered, "I didn't – *honestly* I didn't."

Simon just raised his eyebrows. I could tell he didn't believe me.

"Well, someone did. It's all round the Sixth Form," he said.

Someone, I thought. *And I bet I know who it was.*

I remembered the look Valerie had given me the day before. No wonder she'd looked pleased with herself, stirring up trouble between Simon and me. I didn't have so many friends – guys or girls – that I could afford to lose a couple. For the first time since Valerie had started to have a go at me, I felt a chill of real fear. I'd told Anna and Craig I wouldn't let her get to me. Stupid, childish practical jokes were one thing. Telling lies about me to my friends was something else. If this sort of thing was going to go on, I wasn't sure how long I could handle it. Or even *if* I could handle it. . .

Chapter 6

School was definitely a lot less fun when I didn't have Simon and Paul and the others to go around with. After a week when I hardly spoke to anyone, except Anna at the beginning and end of the day and in a couple of lunch breaks, I had to admit I felt really lonely. Simon was polite, but that was all. He obviously hadn't believed me when I told him that I hadn't been spreading rumours about him and Paul. Heather hardly ever said anything anyway.

And I was always conscious of Valerie and her crowd over at the other side of the common room, laughing, joking, playing music, eating crisps, drinking coffee and Coke, gossiping. . . I didn't want to believe they were gossiping about me.

All the same, it was pretty miserable. I'd given up the idea of being one of the in crowd long ago, but that didn't mean I wanted to be on my own, not part of any crowd at all.

It was all Valerie Maxwell's fault, I thought. If she and her mates hadn't stirred it between Simon and Paul and me, I'd still have had someone to go round with.

Then my gold chain disappeared.

I suppose I was stupid to wear it to school, and even more stupid to take it off when I was changing for gym. But Mark had given it to me on my sixteenth birthday and it was very, very precious to me. I thought of him every time I saw it, remembered his cheeky grin as he'd fastened it round my neck and said, "Here. This is for my favourite sister!" I'd noticed recently that the clasp was a bit loose and kept meaning to go to the jeweller's in town and get it fixed. It sometimes got in the way when we did aerobic warm-ups and I was afraid it'd fly off and get lost, so I took it off and slipped it carefully into my purse when I got changed.

I forgot I wasn't wearing it until I was on my way home, looking in my purse for my bus pass. Then I noticed it wasn't there and my heart began to thump.

Oh, no! I thought. Don't say it's fallen out! But how could it? My purse was closed tight and there was nothing wrong with its fastening. Anything I'd put in there would stay there, safe and sound. And I knew that was where I'd put the chain. So where was it?

Desperately, I turned my school bag out on the seat beside me. The usual clutter fell out – exercise books, textbooks, a file of notes I was taking home, my purse, my little hairbrush, some hand cream, a packet of tissues, half a KitKat . . . but no gold chain.

I don't believe it! I thought. That chain was just about my most precious possession, not because it was that valuable, but because it was almost all I had left of my brother. And now it had disappeared. But how?

Tears sprang to my eyes. I was sure I'd put it carefully into my purse. Could it have slipped out somehow and be among my gym things in my locker at school? I didn't see how, but it seemed like my only hope.

When I looked in my locker the next morning there was no sign of it.

"Are you absolutely sure you left it in your purse?" Anna asked me for about the tenth time.

I was, but you know what it's like when something just seems to disappear like that. You start thinking of the most ridiculous explanations – like maybe I'd just dreamed I'd taken it off and it was still round my neck, or it'd wormed its way out of my purse on to the changing room floor.

We looked all over the changing room, the gym, the Sixth-Form classrooms I'd been in the previous day and the common room, but found nothing.

"We'll have to report it to Miss Latimer," Anna said at last. "She's in charge of Lost Property.

Someone might have handed it in."

Miss Latimer shook her head.

"I'm sorry, Kerry," she said, "but nothing like that has been handed in. Anyway," she looked sternly at me, "you know the rule, don't you? No expensive or precious jewellery at school. If you'd kept it at home, this wouldn't have happened, would it?"

"No, Miss Latimer."

I didn't feel like explaining that there was a special reason why I'd been breaking that particular rule. Wearing that chain made me feel that Mark was closer to me, in a funny sort of way, and now I'd lost it.

It was almost like losing Mark all over again.

Anna put a comforting arm round me when I came out of the office in tears.

"Perhaps it'll turn up," she said forlornly. "You never know. Come back to the common room and have a coffee. You'll feel better."

But when we went into the common room, Valerie, Meg, Judy and the rest of their gang were there, playing a rowdy game of Trivial Pursuit. Amy Flowers glanced over in our direction and gave a huge, noisy sniff.

"All of a sudden there's a funny smell in here," she announced loudly.

Judy and Meg both tittered. Valerie didn't even look up.

"Don't take any notice," Anna whispered. "I'm going to put the kettle on."

A great wave of loneliness washed over me. There I was, among a crowd of people, and it must've been obvious I'd been crying. Not one of them even asked me what the matter was. Not one of them cared.

Anna brought us both a coffee and we sat down to drink it. I happened to be glancing over towards Valerie when she looked up, saw me, and smiled.

It wasn't a friendly, concerned smile. It was a smile of triumph. The smile of someone who'd done something she was proud of, someone who'd got her own way.

A blinding realization suddenly hit me and I almost gasped out loud. She knows something about my missing chain! I thought to myself. Maybe she even stole it herself, from my purse, while we were doing gym. My heart was pounding.

I tried to remember if Valerie had been in the changing room with the rest of us when I'd taken the chain off and put it away. Had she seen me do it? Had she taken it? I got up, almost upsetting my cup of coffee, and walked over to her.

"I've lost my gold chain," I announced.

Valerie raised her eyebrows.

"Gold chain? I didn't know you had one. We're not supposed to wear expensive jewellery to school anyway, you know," she said with mock innocence.

Coming from Valerie, who broke every single school rule she could get away with and then some, I thought that was a cheek.

"I took it off yesterday when I was changing for gym," I went on.

Valerie shrugged. Meg Tate gave me an unfriendly stare and Karen just raised her eyebrows.

"I suppose none of you have seen it anywhere?" I said. "Judy, you did gym with us. Amy, you were there – and you, Valerie. . ."

Valerie didn't say anything, but Judy went red.

"Just a minute," Amy said. "I hope you're not accusing anyone—"

I could be cool too, when I wanted, even when my heart was hammering the way it was now.

"I'm not accusing anyone," I said steadily. "I just want to know where my gold chain is – if any of you have seen it."

Karen and Meg looked away. Judy was still scarlet in the face, Amy looked angry, and Valerie totally blank.

"Sorry," she said carelessly, but there was a malicious light in her dark eyes that I couldn't mistake.

She *does* know something! I thought.

"Well, if you do come across it," I said, "I'd be grateful if you'd let me know. My – my brother gave it to me."

Valerie raised her eyebrows. "Your brother? I didn't know you had a brother."

I shouldn't have told her, I thought.

"I don't any more. He was killed in a car crash," I said.

There was an embarrassed silence. Karen and Meg glanced at one another. No one said anything else and after a moment I went back to Anna and my half-cold coffee.

"They did have something to do with it," I murmured under my breath. "I could swear they did. But I can't prove anything."

I told Craig what had happened and he was really sympathetic. We'd met in one of the locals, since there wasn't anywhere else much to go in town. Julie and Steve had come over too, and we had a really fun evening. There was a karaoke competition which I was much too shy to go in for, but which Julie won, singing one of Madonna's old hits. She had a really good voice as well as the confidence to get up and sing in front of a crowd of people. I'd rather have died, myself.

Steve said he was working an early shift the next morning, so he and Julie had to leave. We finished our drinks and went out into the car park behind the pub to see them off, after making plans to go clubbing at the weekend.

"'Bye! See you on Saturday, then!" I called as Steve drove away.

I turned round, and saw that Craig was talking to a tall guy in leathers who looked vaguely familiar. Another rough-looking bloke was standing beside him.

"What's going on?" I asked.

The first guy turned to me. "Just having a word

with your boyfriend, darling," he said.

I moved closer to Craig, feeling a bit scared. There were two of them, and they looked as if they meant trouble.

"I don't know what all this is about," Craig was protesting.

"Yes, you do. You've offended a friend of mine," said Leather Jacket, with a wolfish grin.

"I have? But what – who—?"

"A lady."

"What lady?" I put in, mystified. What was all this about?

Craig looked as bewildered as I felt.

"Sorry, mate, I haven't a clue what you're talking about," he said. "You must've got the wrong—"

To my horror, Leather Jacket suddenly grabbed Craig and, with his friend's help, pinned him up against the wall.

"Stop it!" I yelled. "What are you doing?"

Craig was helpless, and both men laughed at him as he twisted and struggled to escape.

"I'll get help," I gasped, racing across the car park and in through the side door of the pub.

"Help! Please help!" I shouted. "It's my boyfriend – they're killing him!"

Two or three guys from the bar, including the bouncer, came out with me. We found Craig on his knees beside his car, gasping for breath. I knelt down beside him, terrified.

"Craig, are you hurt? What happened? Where did they go?"

He shook his head.

"I – I'm OK," he managed to stammer out. "They – they didn't hit me, just kept threatening me, then they ran off."

"You OK mate? Can I get you anything? A brandy or anything?" said the pub bouncer.

Craig shook his head.

"No, I – I'm all right. I think they thought I was someone else. They kept going on about some woman I'd upset."

My head jerked up. Suddenly, I remembered where I'd seen the guy in the leather jacket before. *Twice* before, in fact. Once in the chippie in town and the other time outside school, talking to Valerie Maxwell.

Valerie Maxwell! So she was at the bottom of this, too. Not content with virtually ignoring me at school, making trouble for me with Simon and Paul, and stealing my gold chain, now she was setting her biker friends on to Craig!

I started to shiver uncontrollably. This wasn't a joke any more, if it ever had been. It was all very well Anna – and Craig, come to that – telling me to ignore Valerie's spite and not let her get to me, but this was serious. Those guys had meant business with their threats: I could tell they had.

Craig was still looking pale and in the end I did persuade him to come back into the pub for a half of lager. Everything seemed so normal once we got in there, with the bright lights and the music and the conversation. It was hard to believe that just a few metres away the guy I loved had been threatened and almost attacked. And all because of one girl's jealous, vicious spite.

I debated whether to tell Craig I'd recognized the biker – Pete, that was his name. In the end I decided I would. After all, we were in this together.

"Craig, I know that guy – the one who threatened you. He's a friend of Valerie's," I said urgently.

He turned to me, his mouth a round O of surprise.

"You're joking! So that's another of her little games, is it?" he said grimly. "She just doesn't give up, does she?"

I shook my head miserably.

"Right," said Craig, putting his glass down. "That settles it."

"What – what are you going to do?" I quavered nervously. The last thing I wanted was to be in any more trouble than I already was.

Craig smiled reassuringly at me and kissed the tip of my nose.

"Don't worry," he said. "Everything's going to be all right, you'll see."

"Really?"

"I promise."

I settled back, loving the feeling of his arms round me. At least Craig's on my side, I thought happily. Whatever Valerie did, or tried to do, I still had Craig, and Anna, and my family.

* * *

I needed that feeling to carry me through the next few days at school, which were really awful. Anna spent most of her time in the labs and that meant I was left alone. And I mean alone. It was horrible in the common room when everyone else was in little groups and cliques. Of course I pretended not to care, but I did. It was the way Valerie's crowd seemed to stop talking when I came into the room, or else looked over my way and started laughing, as if they knew something I didn't know. I was early for one of our English Literature lessons and when I arrived in the classroom someone had written KERRY GILBERT IS A SLAG on the blackboard in huge letters. I grabbed the eraser and rubbed it off before anyone saw, but it still made me feel awful.

Then, one day, just before I went home, I was in the loo when I heard the cloakroom door open and a couple of girls, maybe three, came in. They were washing their hands and doing their hair and chatting and I recognized the voices of Meg, Amy and Karen.

Suddenly, I heard Craig's name mentioned. I strained my ears.

"Yes," Meg – or was it Karen? – was saying, "he called her last night. She hadn't heard from him for months."

I heard a gasp from Amy.

"So has he finished with Kerry, then? Is he going back to Valerie?"

"Who knows? He definitely wanted to meet her, she said."

The cloakroom door creaked open and I heard footsteps and chatter dying away in the distance.

I felt sick. I could hardly believe what I'd heard. Craig had telephoned Valerie and wanted to see her. That's what they'd said.

Did they know I was listening? Was it just a wind-up, put on for my benefit, or had he really rung her?

"Calm down," Anna advised. I'd managed to catch her just before her bus went and explain what I'd heard.

"If it's true that Craig rang Valerie, it was probably just to tell her to back off and leave the two of you alone."

"You really think so?"

"Well, it's the most likely explanation, isn't it? You said he was mad when you told him that biker type was a friend of hers."

I heaved a huge sigh. What Anna said made sense. Craig probably *was* trying to reason with Valerie, explain yet again that the two of them were through and had been for months. But I still didn't like it.

"When are you seeing him again?" Anna said practically.

"Tomorrow, I think."

"Well, ask him straight out, then you'll know. But I honestly don't think you have a thing to worry about," she added comfortingly.

I planned to ring Craig as soon as I got home.

When I arrived at our place, though, Dad's car was in the drive and the front door was open.

"Dad? Mum?" I said as I walked through the door. "What's going on?"

Then I stifled a scream as a strange man came down the stairs towards me. Behind him was my dad, looking worried to death.

"Kerry?" he said.

"Dad? What is it? Where's Mum?"

The stranger shook my hand.

"I'm Dr Garside," he said. "It's all right, Kerry, your mother will be fine."

"Mum?" I echoed. "Is she – what's the matter?"

Dad put his arm round my shoulders and led me into the living room. I sat on the sofa and Dr Garside in one of the armchairs. Jessie came and rested her nose on my knee, whining softly.

"Your mum's ill, Kerry," Dr Garside said gently.

"Ill? But—"

"I can't be sure at this stage, but I think she's suffering from severe clinical depression," he went on.

"Depression," I echoed. I knew Mum was depressed. She had been, ever since Mark was killed. It had seemed to hit her harder than either Dad or me. We'd both hoped that moving would take her out of herself, give her something new to think about, help her to come to terms with losing Mark. But it hadn't, not really. Dad had his new job to think about, I had school, and Craig, and everything. Mum was taking some tablets Dr Garside, our new GP, had prescribed, but I knew she wasn't happy. How long is it, I thought, since I saw Mum smile, heard her laugh?

I nodded slowly.

"So . . . what's going to happen to Mum?" I asked anxiously. "She's been taking those pills. Aren't they doing any good?"

The doctor was silent for a moment.

"I've been talking to your dad," he said, "and we both feel that, since the tablets your mum's been taking haven't helped that much, it might be best if she came into hospital for a while."

"Hospital?" I gasped.

"Oh, it won't be for long," the doctor said hastily. "Just so that one of my colleagues can have a look at her – there's an excellent psychiatric unit attached to the hospital – and find out what kind of treatment would suit her best. Once we find her the right medication, she'll be able to come home, don't worry."

I couldn't take it in. My mum was going into a *psychiatric unit*?

I burst into tears.

"You mean Mum's losing her mind? Having some sort of nervous breakdown?" I sobbed.

Dad came over and put his arm round me.

"Ssh, Kerry," he said. "Mum's severely depressed. You know she hasn't been her usual self since Mark died. Dr Garside has been explaining to me that they have all kinds of new drugs these days that can help her. You're not to worry, she'll get better."

I scrubbed at my eyes with a tissue.

"But why now?" I said. "I mean. . ."

Dad smiled sadly. "Have you thought what the date is, Kerry?"

I thought.

"It's the eighteenth of October. Why – *oh!*"

I hadn't forgotten, truly I hadn't, but with all the trouble at school it had got pushed to the back of my mind. Tomorrow, the nineteenth of October, was – would have been – my brother Mark's twentieth birthday.

No wonder Mum was depressed, here alone at home while Dad was out at work and I was at school. Alone with her memories.

"Oh Dad!" I whispered.

"Well," Dad said, "your mum just couldn't cope. The lady next door saw the bedroom curtains drawn at lunch-time and heard Jessie whining, so she phoned me, and I found your mum in bed."

"She hadn't—?"

Surely, *surely* Mum wouldn't try to kill herself? Not while she knew Dad I still loved her, needed her?

"No," said Dr Garside, "she hadn't taken an overdose or anything, but she wouldn't get up so your dad very wisely called the surgery."

"I'm going to drive her over to the hospital now," Dad said gently, "but we wanted to wait till you came home so that we could explain what had happened."

"I'm coming with you," I said.

"No need," said Dr Garside. "I've given your mum something to calm her down. I promise you she'll get better."

It was hard to believe that as Dad and the doctor helped Mum downstairs. Her face was expressionless and when I gave her a hug her body was quite rigid.

"Get well soon, Mum," I whispered. "We love you!"

Mum managed a sad little smile as the doctor led her away.

The house seemed hideously empty without Mum and Dad. If it hadn't been for Jessie, I don't know what I would have done. She climbed up beside me on the sofa and put one paw on my knee, looking up at me with huge, liquid eyes full of doggy sympathy.

"Oh Jessie!" I whispered. "What are we going to do?"

The telephone rang and I raced to pick it up. It was Anna.

"Well," she said, "have you spoken to him yet?"

I couldn't think what she was talking about.

"Have I . . . who?" I said vaguely.

"Craig, you dummy! Have you asked him if he rang Valerie or not?"

It seemed like about a year since I'd been at school, overhearing the others talk about Craig and Valerie.

"No, I. . ." I said.

"Kerry?" came Anna's voice. "What is it? What's the matter? Are you all right?"

"No, not really," I said. "It's Mum. She's in hospital."

I heard Anna's gasp at the other end of the line.

"But what happened? What's wrong with her?"

I told her what Dad and Dr Garside had said.

"Oh Kerry," she breathed, "that's awful! Your poor mum! But try not to worry. They think she's going to be all right, don't they?"

I nodded, and then realized that Anna couldn't see me.

"Kerry? Are you still there?"

Suddenly my throat was so choked up I could hardly speak.

"I – I'm here," I croaked.

There was a pause and then Anna said, "I'm coming over. Dad or Mum will drive me, I know they will. Can I stay at yours tonight?"

I couldn't imagine anything better than Anna, kind, sensible Anna, coming over to spend the night.

"Please come, Anna," I begged.

"I'll be with you as soon as I can," she said, and rang off.

I fed Jessie and made up the spare bed in my room, and by the time I'd done that the front door bell was ringing.

Anna gave me a big hug.

"You poor thing," she commiserated. "What an awful shock."

"Yes, it was," I said. "But I – we – should have thought. It would have been my brother's birthday tomorrow, I think that was what really upset Mum."

"Oh Kerry," said Anna, "I – I don't know what to say. I've never really lost anyone I loved. My Grandad Sheldon died before I was born so I never knew him."

I didn't care if Anna saw me cry.

"I really loved him, Anna," I sobbed. "He was – he was such a great guy. I couldn't bear it when people started saying all those awful things about him."

Anna looked bewildered.

"Awful things?"

"Well, about the crash, and that poor little girl. . ."

Anna just looked blankly at me. Then I remembered, to my horror, that I hadn't ever told her the full story of Mark's accident. She didn't know about the stolen car, the joy-riding, the child who had died. So I told her.

Afterwards, there was an awful silence.

"Oh Kerry!" she said in a shaken voice. "How sad. How desperately sad. No wonder your mum can't cope."

"That's why we moved up here, away from London," I went on. "Everyone knew us there. People pointed at us in the street, and someone wrote KILLER on our garden wall. It was a nightmare."

Anna nodded slowly.

"So we came up here to start a new life," I said. "I don't think anyone knows about Mark — except you, now. You won't tell anyone, will you?"

"Of course not!" she said indignantly.

"Promise?"

"I promise."

Chapter 7

If it hadn't been for Anna, I don't know how I would have got through the next few days. She stuck to me like glue at school, dashing over from the lab in between lessons so I didn't have to be by myself too much. Everyone else more or less ignored me. Valerie's crowd seemed to have given up their stupid, snide comments, which was something. Now, they just acted like I didn't exist at all.

There was one awful moment when Miss Latimer called to me at the end of an English lesson.

"Kerry, I'd like a word with you, please," she said.

I saw Meg and Karen raise their eyebrows and smirk at one another. My heart started to thump. Now what was coming?

But Miss Latimer was looking sympathetic.

"I just wanted to say that I'm sorry to hear about your mother, Kerry," she said.

I gasped. "Oh! How – how did you—?"

"Your father rang the Head to let us know."

My mind was in a whirl. Why hadn't Dad said anything to me? I knew he was sick with worry about Mum, of course. I hated seeing him like that. It didn't seem like him to let strangers know our private business.

"Don't look like that," said Miss Latimer gently. "We're not interfering, Kerry, but as teachers, we do need to know if any of the students have problems at home. Then we can make allowances."

"I – I suppose so. Thanks, Miss Latimer," I said. I still felt dazed.

"If you need someone to talk to, you know where I am," she said.

I wasn't sure what to say. Miss Latimer was OK, as teachers go, but there was no way I could've confided in her about Mum, or Mark, or anything else really. She was a *teacher*.

"Um . . . thank you," I mumbled.

"And try not to worry too much. I'm sure she'll be fine. She's in the best place!" she called brightly, as I stuffed my books in my bag and headed for the door.

I almost collided with Meg and Karen, hanging around outside. Earwigging, I bet, I thought angrily. The last thing I needed was for Valerie and her gang to get hold of the news that my mum was in the local psychiatric unit. I could just imagine what they'd make of that.

I told Craig about Mum's depression when we

met later that evening. Just like Anna, he couldn't have been more sympathetic. For about the thousandth time, I thought how lucky I was to have him. Then I remembered to ask him about his phone call to Valerie.

"I told you I'd sort it out, didn't I?" he said, slipping his arm round my shoulders and giving me a comforting hug.

"Yes, but what—?"

"I told her we knew what she was up to, that you recognized those guys that had a go at me in the car park, and that if she tried anything like that again I'd report it to the police," said Craig firmly.

I was silent. I wanted Craig to be firm, but I wasn't sure how Valerie would respond.

"I also told her to leave you alone," Craig went on. "I said that as far as I was concerned, she and I were through, that I was seeing you now, and that was all there was to it."

"And what did she say?"

"Not much she could say, was there?"

All the same, I couldn't see Valerie giving up. She wanted Craig back, she'd told me that. She'd also said that she always got what she wanted. And I had the feeling she'd stop at nothing.

"She – she scares me, Craig," I admitted. "I'm not even sure that this is about wanting to go out with you again."

He kissed the end of my nose.

"How many times do I have to tell you? There's absolutely no chance of that," he said.

"I know. But Valerie doesn't see it like that. It's a sort of weird power struggle with her. She wants to be in control."

"Well, she can't control us," said Craig, "so let's forget about her, OK?"

We made plans to go out at the weekend with Julie and Steve and I tried to put Valerie to the back of my mind. It was hard, though. I'd wanted to make a fresh start in my new school and here I was, left out, ignored, treated like a bit of dirt. And all because of one girl.

There was good news about Mum, though. Dr Garside told us she was responding well to the anti-depressants they'd put her on and she was also going to talk to a bereavement counsellor who, he said, would help her to come to terms with what had happened. Soon she would be able to come home.

Then I found my gold chain at the back of my locker at school.

"Anna!" I shrieked. "Look what I've found! It's my chain – you know, the one Mark gave me."

Anna looked amazed.

"But where on earth did you find it?"

"At the back of my locker."

"Your locker? But – but we looked there when it first went missing, Kerry. We went over and over it. How on earth could we have missed seeing it?"

It was strange, no doubt about it. That chain hadn't been in my locker before, I could swear it hadn't. Now it had suddenly reappeared.

"There's only one explanation," I said grimly. "The person who took it wasn't a thief, just a wind-up merchant – and I think we can both guess who *that* points to!"

Anna was looking troubled.

"D'you think you should report it?"

I was struggling with the clasp as I fixed it round my neck again, where it belonged.

"Why bother? I've got it back, that's all that matters to me. I'm going to get the clasp mended and then I'm going to keep it safely in my jewellery box at home."

Finding the chain, plus the good news about Mum, cheered me up no end.

When I arrived at school the following morning, Paul and Simon were in the common room making coffee.

"Hi," I said. Things weren't anything like back to normal with those two, but we were at least on speaking terms. Any rumours that there had been about them seemed to have died down. I was hoping we could be friends again, one day.

"Hello, Kerry," Paul mumbled. Simon just nodded.

What's wrong with them now? I thought, exasperated.

Heather came in, saw me, blushed scarlet, and scuttled out again like a scared rabbit.

I was looking through the project I was doing for

Sociology, which was due to be handed in, when the door opened again. It was Valerie Maxwell. She swaggered over and stood right in front of me, her hands on her hips and a mocking smile on her face.

"Well," she said softly, "you *are* a dark horse, aren't you, Kerry?"

"What do you want, Valerie?" I said wearily. I didn't want to start some sort of slanging match first thing in the morning.

She shrugged.

"Me? I don't want anything. Just a chat."

I didn't like the sound of that at all.

"What d'you mean, a chat?"

"About your family," said Valerie loudly.

"My *family*?"

Meg and Amy had come in and were standing behind Valerie. I tried to stay calm but I couldn't help feeling threatened.

"Shut up, Valerie," said Simon suddenly. "It's no business of ours, anyway."

"Oh, but it is," said Valerie silkily. "All this term we've had to put up with Kerry Gilbert swanning around the place as if she owned it—"

"I did not!" I protested.

"Leave her alone," said Paul.

"Is it true your mother's in a mental hospital?" said Judy Priestly.

Oh, *no!* I thought. I might've known they'd find out! In such a small town, everyone knows everyone else's business.

I looked Judy straight in the eye.

"Yes," I said. "She's in the psychiatric unit being treated for depression. The doctors say she can come home in a week or two. OK?"

I could have explained about Mark's birthday, but I didn't feel like it. Anyway, I thought indignantly, why should I? Simon was quite right – it wasn't anyone else's business.

Judy, at least, had the grace to look a bit embarrassed.

"Anything else you want to know?" I asked her coolly.

She didn't say anything, just backed away with Meg and Karen, none of them meeting my eyes.

But Valerie still stood in front of me.

"It must run in the family," she said, so softly that none of the others could hear. "Mental illness, I mean. *I* wouldn't fancy having a mother who was a loony—"

That was when I lost it. I've had enough! I thought. I jumped up and slapped Valerie hard across the face.

"You bitch!" I yelled. "How *dare* you call my mother names! Who d'you think you are, Valerie Maxwell? It's time someone told you you're not the only person who matters in the world. You've done your best to make my life hell ever since I came here, just because my boyfriend dumped you. You're an evil, jealous cow!"

I was shaking with fury. I'd never flown at anyone like that in my life before, never even wanted to. I'd listened to Anna and Craig's advice, I'd tried to ignore Valerie, I'd put up with her taunts and her spite for long enough on my own behalf. But everyone has a breaking-point, and when she started on Mum, that was it. I was glad I'd slapped her. I really felt I could've killed her.

There was a deadly silence in the common room. I think the others were too amazed to say or do anything. I could see the red marks made by my fingers across Valerie's smooth olive cheeks. I was glad I'd hurt her.

Suddenly, she spoke.

"You'll be sorry you did that, Kerry," she said. She spoke quite quietly but her voice was so full of venom that I started to shake.

Then she turned round and walked out of the room.

When Valerie had gone the others seemed to come to life. No one actually said anything to me. Valerie's cronies were in a little huddle on the other side of the room, muttering to each other and glancing over in my direction from time to time. I heard Simon say "She asked for it!" and then the bell went for first lesson.

I felt sick and shaky and wished I could go home, or at the very least, find Anna and talk it all over with her.

Valerie didn't appear for the rest of the morning. I didn't know where she'd gone. I saw Anna at lunch-time, and when I told her I'd actually thumped Valerie she grinned and said, "Good for

118

you!" But she still looked worried – almost as worried as I felt.

Now what would Valerie do? Somehow, I knew that from now on it was open warfare between us. I'd have to watch my back.

"She can't do anything," Craig said confidently. "There are too many people around at school for her to have a go at you there, and when you go out, I shall be with you. Don't worry."

"Thanks," I said gratefully. "I don't know, Craig – maybe I shouldn't have lashed out like that, but—"

"It'll teach her a lesson. Show her she can push you just so far," Craig said reassuringly.

All the same, I still felt nervous and jumpy even walking across the school grounds between lessons, if I was on my own. Valerie's crowd were still ignoring me. Some of the others asked me a couple of times how Mum was. They sounded embarrassed. Craig and Anna were great, though, and that made up for a lot.

Then, one night, I'd stayed late for a drama group meeting, and when I went to catch the bus I was just in time to see its tail-lights disappear round the corner of Stoneleigh Road.

Oh, no! I thought. It was half an hour before the next bus and I didn't fancy hanging around that long. If I walked fast, I could be home in twenty minutes.

I set off up the dusky, silent streets, wishing the

school was nearer the centre of town and that there weren't so many houses with big, deserted gardens full of tall, looming shrubs, where anyone could hide. It was a murky, drizzly evening and I pulled my scarf and coat around me, shivering as I hurried along.

I heard the crack of a branch snapping and my heart leapt into my throat. Was there someone lurking behind the bushes? I couldn't tell.

I could see the lights of the dual-carriageway ahead of me. I only had to cross the footbridge, walk past the park and turn into Brompton Drive, then into our street. Just another ten minutes' walking and I'd be safe.

I thought of Jessie, waiting at home for me. I thought of Dad, working so hard in his new job, all the time worried to death about Mum. She'd be home soon, hopefully a lot more like her old self. I couldn't bear the idea of Mark's death tearing my whole family apart.

I thought of Craig, lovely Craig. At least *something*'s gone right in my new life, I thought gratefully. I've got the kind of boyfriend I never, ever thought I'd find. And a good friend too, in Anna.

What was that? Three muffled figures came out of a side road and stood directly in front of me. They were girls – I was sure of that, they weren't tall enough to be guys – but they had scarves and hats on so I couldn't swear it was anyone I knew. I thought I recognized Meg Tate's black coat . . .

and wasn't that Karen Connor's distinctive red hair I could see tucked under a dark-coloured hat?

"What d'you want?" I said more confidently than I felt, as they were blocking my path.

No one said anything.

I tried to walk on, push through them, and then felt a shove in the small of my back that sent me sprawling into the gutter. My school bag went flying and I felt something – a boot, probably – catch my shoulder a glancing blow.

Muggers! I thought as I lay there, terrified, curling my arms round my head to protect it. Oh, no! What are they going to do to me? I haven't got any money.

I felt another cruel blow smash into my ribs and almost blacked out with the pain. I heard a groan and realized that it was me. Then a voice – was it one I recognized? – called "Enough!" and I heard footsteps running away.

For a few moments I just lay there, winded. Then, very slowly, very cautiously, I sat up, wincing. My bag was a few metres away. I got slowly to my feet, hobbled over to it and picked it up. It hadn't even been opened, so nothing was missing.

They weren't muggers, then, I thought, tears springing to my eyes. I wasn't a random target. I'd been chosen, deliberately, as a victim. And it wasn't hard to guess who by.

Somehow, I managed to get home, peel off my wet clothes, and crawl into a hot bath. My tights were ruined, my school skirt was soaked and I was bruised all over, with one long graze on my leg. I lay in the hot, scented water, tears of shock and weariness streaming down my cheeks.

So much for starting a new life! I thought tiredly. It's every bit as bad out here as it was in London. It seems as though everywhere I go, there are people who hate me and want to make my life a misery. I can't stand it.

"Kerry? What in the world have you done to yourself?" Dad said when he came home. I was in my dressing-gown, still looking battered and bruised and feeling sick and miserable.

For a moment I was tempted to tell Dad all about it. Perhaps he could do something, or the school. . .

But then I thought of Valerie Maxwell's reaction if she knew I'd grassed, and shuddered. If my life was hell now, what would it be like after that?

No, I couldn't tell Dad. Anyway, he had enough to worry about with Mum. This was something I had to sort out myself.

"I fell over," I said. "Slipped on some wet leaves on my way home. I've given my ribs a bit of a bashing."

"Let me see."

I showed Dad the bruises and he was horrified, but seemed to accept my story that I'd had a bad fall. He put some ointment on them and tucked me up in bed with a bowl of tomato soup and some toast, just as if I was a little girl again. Jessie came and sat comfortingly on the bed beside me, her nose resting on her paws.

Dad made me stay off school the next day. Then I went back and carried on as if nothing had happened. I'd told Anna, of course, and Craig, but there was nothing any of us could do. I'd thought I'd recognized Meg's coat and Karen's red hair, but that was all. Once, I caught Valerie looking at me with a smug gleam in her dark eyes, but that didn't prove anything either. Mostly, they all just ignored me, as before.

Oh, there were little annoyances, like my best pen disappearing as mysteriously as my gold chain had done, Amy Flowers tripping me up in gym class and swearing it was an accident, inkstains appearing on my new sports bag, someone writing NUTTER on a piece of paper and slipping it into my desk, loud remarks being made whenever Anna and I came into the room, but no one actually attacked me again.

"To think we thought she might have given up!" I said miserably to Craig.

Even he was looking worried by this time. He'd been furious when I told him about the attack and made me promise never to walk home alone again, even if it meant waiting an hour for the bus.

"Oh God, Kerry! I'm sorry," he said. "I feel as if half of this is my fault, anyway."

"Your fault? How can it be?"

"If I'd known that Valerie was going to terrorize

123

the next person I went out with . . . I wish to God I'd never gone out with her at all!"

"It's not your fault," I assured him. "She's crazy, and the craziest thing is, she thinks this is the way to get you back."

When I felt really down, I even thought about splitting up with Craig, or at least pretending to, just to see if that would calm her down.

"It won't," Craig said gloomily. "Even if you and I really did split up, I'd never, ever go back to her, especially not after this. Anyway, I don't see why we should let her split us up. You're the best thing that's ever happened to me, Kerry."

I hugged him tight.

"So are you," I assured him.

He took my hand and held it tightly in his.

"We're not going to let her pull us apart, Kerry," he said. "We're not, are we?"

My hand looked small and pale next to his big tanned one. I managed a watery smile and held on more tightly.

"No," I said firmly. "Together, we're strong. Stronger than Valerie, stronger than anyone."

"Together," he echoed.

Mum came home from hospital the following week. She looked fragile and tired and was still seeing her counsellor and taking loads of pills, but she seemed a lot more like her old self.

"You've got to let Kerry and me know what we can do to help, love," Dad said, taking her hands.

"I blame myself, you know. I should have noticed how bad you were feeling. I should have thought about Mark's birthday."

"It's good to have you home, Mum," I told her. "It was awful without you."

"Your dad tells me you've managed very well," Mum said. "And things are still OK with Craig, aren't they? And that nice Anna?"

I nodded. If only you knew! I thought.

"Good," said Mum with a ghost of her old smile. "I'm so glad you've made friends, Kerry. It's not always easy, settling down in a new town."

You're telling me! I thought.

At school that week Valerie, Meg and Karen were full of the weekend trip they'd made to London. They'd been to Camden Lock and Portobello Road and out clubbing every night. Valerie, at least, had come back with tonnes of new clothes and, according to Karen, had pulled an incredibly good-looking guy. She would! I thought, but I didn't say anything. London, and the life I'd led there, seemed like a million years ago. I didn't even feel envious. London made me think about Mark, and even after all these months, it still hurt. My life was here now, with Craig, and Anna, Mum and Dad – and Jessie.

I was only half-listening when Valerie and the others were talking about their trip to Judy and Amy, who'd stayed at home. It was only when I heard my name mentioned that my attention was really grabbed.

Meg had lowered her voice but I could still hear her. I looked over at the gossiping crowd and sighed to myself, expecting some bitchy comment at any moment.

Judy's eyes were like saucers.

"Are you sure it's true?" she was saying.

Meg and Valerie both nodded.

"No wonder she hardly ever talks about him," said Karen in a loud voice.

Valerie looked up, caught my eye, and said casually, "How come you didn't tell us about your brother, Kerry?"

I felt cold inside.

"I – I *have* told you about my brother. He was killed in a car crash in January," I said.

"How sad!" purred Valerie.

She can't have found out about Mark! I thought desperately. *She can't.*

"Yes, it was awful," I said.

"It must have been," Valerie went on, her voice dripping with sympathy. At least, if I hadn't known her better, that was what I would've thought.

"*Especially* sad when you found out he was a joy-rider, driving a stolen car," the velvet voice went on. "And fancy! He jumped a red light and crashed into a mini-cab, killing a little girl!"

There was deadly silence in the common room. Five pairs of eyes looked at me, appalled – except for Valerie Maxwell, who looked as though she'd won the National Lottery.

"Isn't it tragic," Valerie continued. "It must be

awful, being a killer's sister. I don't think I could bear to live with it, myself. No wonder your mother went out of her mind."

Oh, no! I thought. *Oh, NO!*

It felt like the end of the world.

It *was* the end – the end of all our hopes of starting a new life, away from everyone who had known us, and known Mark.

Valerie Maxwell knew.

She'd told the rest of her cronies, and that meant it'd be all round the Sixth Form by the end of the day, and all round the school by tomorrow. I remembered how it had been at my school in London – people avoiding me, pointing at me in the street, in the corridors, in the canteen.

Now it was all going to happen again and there was nothing I could do about it, no way I could escape. Nowhere to run.

My past, the awful secret I had thought I'd left behind me for ever, had caught up with me, and nothing could ever be the same again. I'd be branded for ever as the killer's sister. Valerie Maxwell would see to that. What was more, she would enjoy it.

"Is it true, Kerry?" said Karen, in a hushed voice.

I nodded. There was no point in lying. My brother – my stupid, reckless, thoughtless brother – *had* driven a stolen car, *had* crashed it, *had* killed that poor little girl.

He'd paid for it with his own life, and it looked

as though I was going to have to pay for Mark's stupidity for the rest of mine.

I bowed my head, not wanting Karen, Valerie and the others to see me cry. The bell went for the start of afternoon school but I just sat there, unable to move, as the others got their things together and went off to their first lessons. I couldn't face them. I couldn't face anyone. Because I'd just thought of something else.

How could Valerie have found out about Mark? I hadn't even told Craig exactly how my brother had died. There was only one person who knew, one person I'd confided in, and she had promised faithfully not to say anything.

She must have betrayed me.

My best friend, Anna.

Chapter 8

"Hey, Kerry! Wait for me!"

Anna came flying down the school steps just as I was hurrying off to catch the bus at the end of the afternoon. All I wanted to do was get away, go home, go up to my bedroom and cry my troubles away. Not that it would do any good.

I'd had a free period that afternoon and I'd sat in the library, a book of nineteenth-century poetry in front of me, not taking in a single word I was supposed to be reading. I couldn't concentrate. I couldn't think about anything except Valerie Maxwell's spiteful face when she'd looked at me and called me a killer's sister. How had she found out?

The only person I'd told was Anna. Even Craig didn't know. And here was Anna, bouncing along beside me, slightly out of breath, her schoolbag in her arms, smiling as if she hadn't a care in the world. Didn't she *know* what she'd done? I thought bitterly. How could she be so stupid?

"Kerry?" Anna was saying. "Are you all right? What's up?"

I looked at her. She was looking totally innocent.

For a moment, I wavered. Perhaps I'd got the wrong end of the stick. But how could I have? Anna was the only person who knew, so it must've been Anna who had given the game away.

"Kerry?" Anna repeated, her smile fading. "What is it? Tell me."

"It's Valerie Maxwell," I began.

Anna sighed and tried to link her arm through mine. I pulled away abruptly.

"I might have known," she said. "What's she done now?"

I took a deep breath and looked her straight in the eyes.

"She knows about Mark," I said.

Anna looked horrified. Her eyes widened and she gave a little gasp.

"Oh, no!" she said. "You mean – you mean about the accident and everything . . . the stolen car . . . that poor little girl who died?"

I nodded. I couldn't even speak.

"Oh Kerry, that's awful! I can just imagine what she said. Oh, poor you! What are you going to do?"

"I don't know," I said through gritted teeth. "But what I want to know is, how did she find out?"

Our eyes met. Anna was looking totally blank.

"I can't. . ." she began.

I carried on staring at her. It was as though I'd never seen her before. Anna, my best friend. My *only* friend.

A blush slowly simmered up from her neck to her face and she took a step backwards.

"You don't think *I* told her?" she gasped. "Kerry, I – I wouldn't—"

"I don't know what I think," I said flatly.

"But I promised!"

"I know you did."

Anna stepped back again, her mouth trembling, hugging her schoolbag to her chest as if she was trying to protect herself.

"You – you *do* think it was me," she whispered. "I can tell you do. You know I hate Valerie Maxwell as much as you do, you know I'm your friend, you know I promised never to tell anyone what you'd told me about Mark. And now you're accusing me—"

"You're the only person I told. The only person who knew," I said stubbornly, avoiding her eyes. "What am I supposed to think? If you didn't tell Valerie, who did?"

Anna was crying, big tears splashing down from under her glasses. She didn't even try to wipe them away. I didn't say anything, bitterness and hurt churning away inside me until I wanted to scream out loud. I'd thought Anna was my friend. I'd trusted her. Apart from Craig, she was the only person I did trust.

And she'd betrayed me, she must have done. There wasn't any other explanation.

When I looked up again, Anna had gone, mingling with a crowd of Fifth-Formers who'd just come out of the Biology lab. I turned round and walked off towards the bus stop on my own.

This is how it's going to be from now on, I thought drearily. Just me, all alone. No friends, no one to talk to, no one to have a laugh with. Branded for ever as a killer's sister.

I didn't know how I was going to be able to bear it.

From then on, things just got worse.

"Oh, look! It's the gangster's moll," said Karen Connor as I came into the common room next day. She and the others screamed with laughter. Anna, who was the only other person there, just looked straight through me as if I didn't exist. Valerie looked from her to me and then back to her again and then raised her eyebrows in a knowing sort of way.

"Had a row, then, have we?" she said smugly.

Anna got up and went out of the room without a word.

"Even old Four-Eyes can't cope with being mates with a killer's sister," sniggered Meg Tate.

"What about lover-boy?" Valerie murmured quietly to me. "Does he know what sort of family he's got himself mixed up in? I bet he doesn't."

"Why don't you mind your own business?" I muttered.

"But it *is* my business," said Valerie smoothly. "Craig Shaw's an old friend of mine. Maybe someone ought to warn him."

"He – he already knows," I lied desperately.

Valerie raised her eyebrows.

"Does he, now? I'm afraid I just don't believe you."

My heart was hammering.

"Of course," Valerie went on, "if you dumped him. . ."

"Dumped him?"

Her dark eyes were gleaming with malice.

"If you told him you didn't want to see him any more . . . well, he need never know your nasty little secret."

"You mean—?"

She grinned. "I really don't think I can let an old friend like Craig – and such a nice guy, too – not know what kind of girl he's going out with. A liar and a killer's sister. Poor old Craig!"

"But – but that's blackmail!" I whispered. "You're telling me that if I don't tell Craig about Mark—"

"Then I will," she said sweetly.

"You – you can't do that. I—"

"Can't I? Just watch me. I told you ages ago, Kerry, I always get what I want. And I happen to want Craig Shaw. It's as simple as that."

"But—"

She shrugged. "It's up to you, Kerry. Dump Craig, and I won't say a word about your brother to him or anyone else. I promise."

"And if I don't?"

"Then I'll make sure everyone in town who matters knows. And that includes Craig. OK? It's your choice, Kerry."

My head was spinning as I sat on the bus home that night. What on earth could I do? I knew Valerie well enough by now to know that she was perfectly capable of carrying out her threat. She'd tell Craig – and everyone else.

And if she did, what would he do? Would he dump me, refuse to have anything to do with a girl whose brother was a joy-rider and child-killer? Would he blame me for not telling him about Mark before? Would he think I didn't love him, didn't trust him enough to share my awful secret with him? I've got to tell him, I thought determinedly. Before Valerie does.

I hated talking about Mark. I'd told Craig that he had died in a car crash, but I hadn't given him all the details. Why? *Because I was ashamed.* I hated being a killer's sister. Oh, I trusted Craig, I knew – I *hoped* – he'd understand, but that didn't make it any easier.

I had a date with Craig the following evening, so I had just twenty-four hours to decide. It felt like the longest twenty-four hours of my life. I hardly slept, I didn't want any breakfast, I couldn't concentrate on my work and Miss Latimer had a go at me in English for "daydreaming".

If only she knew! I thought, biting back the tears.

I wasn't daydreaming. My life was more like a nightmare.

Anna ignored me and so did everyone else, except Valerie, who kept giving me knowing looks. My stomach churned every time I caught her eye. My fate was in her hands and she knew it. She was loving every minute of it, I could tell.

By dinner time I felt really, really sick. I made an excuse to Mum, told her I didn't want any dinner because Craig was taking me out for a pizza later. I wore the green shirt that I knew Craig liked. After all, I thought, my eyes blurring with tears, this might be our very last date.

I might never see Craig again after tonight. . .

"You're quiet this evening. Is anything wrong?" he smiled as he brought the drinks to our table.

My heart lurched. Now was my chance to tell Craig everything. I owed him that, at least. And if he didn't want to know me afterwards, well, at least I'd told him, and it would be the whole truth, not some garbled gossip from Valerie.

I took a deep breath.

"Craig," I said, "there's something I – I have to tell you."

He took a long drink of his lager.

"Go on then," he said casually, "what is it?"

Then he saw my hands were trembling and his smile faded.

"What is it, Kerry?" he repeated. "What's the matter?"

So I told him.

Afterwards, there was a long silence. I hardly dared to look at him. In fact, I hardly dared to breathe. I was half-expecting him to get up and walk right out of the pub, leaving me stranded. When two warm, strong hands gripped mine across the pub table and Craig's voice said "Oh Kerry, how *awful!*" I could hardly believe my ears.

At last, I looked up. Instead of the shock or even revulsion I'd expected to see on his face, all I could see was concern . . . and kindness . . . and, yes, love.

"You poor thing!" said Craig tenderly. "You should've told me before, Kerry. That was why your mum got so depressed, wasn't it? It was more than just the accident, and losing Mark."

I nodded. "Y-yes, it was," I said. "It was horrible when we lived in London, Craig. Everyone knew, and someone wrote KILLER on the wall outside our house. It was a complete nightmare."

"It must have been," he said sympathetically. "I'm glad you told me, Kerry. It can't have been easy for you. I won't tell anyone."

To my horror, the tears that I'd been holding back all day suddenly spilled from my eyes and poured down my cheeks. I should have known, I thought. I should have trusted Craig to understand.

He slid along the bench seat and put his arm round me.

"Hey, don't cry," he said softly. "I'm here . . . it's all right. I'm sorry about your brother, I really am."

"I – I loved him, Craig," I wept. "He was always a bit of a tearaway, we all knew that, but I still loved him. He was such a laugh I don't think any of us could believe he would ever do anything so stupid."

"Ssh!" said Craig.

I gulped and tried to calm down, before I remembered that I hadn't told Craig everything.

"But – but that's not all," I went on. "Valerie Maxwell knows."

Craig frowned. "Valerie? Surely you didn't tell *her*?"

"No, I didn't. My friend – at least I thought she was my friend – Anna told her."

"But why?"

I shrugged. "Just couldn't keep her mouth shut, I suppose."

"And what did Valerie say?"

I took another deep breath, feeling much calmer.

"She told me that unless I dumped you, she'd tell you – and everyone else in town as well."

I had never seen Craig look so angry. His lips narrowed to a thin line and his eyes were like chips of blue ice.

"Stupid cow!" he said venomously. "Does she really think that I'd go back to her, even if you and I finished?"

"She obviously thought you'd dump me if she told you about Mark. That's why I got in first, before she had the chance," I said.

"I hope you didn't think that," Craig said

roughly. "I love you, Kerry. I've never felt like this about anyone else. I want to be with you. I don't care what your brother may or may not have done. None of it was your fault."

"No," I whispered, my emotions see-sawing crazily between fear and a wild, unbelievable happiness. Craig loved me! He actually said he loved me. He'd never said that to me before — no one had.

"I love you too, Craig," I said.

I had never been so certain of anything. The world had suddenly started to look like a completely different place. I'd been lost, lonely, not knowing where to turn or who to confide in — and now, here was Craig, loving, caring, looking out for me. As long as he was on my side, I knew I'd be all right.

Craig took another sip of his beer.

"So Valerie's still giving you a hard time, then," he said thoughtfully.

I nodded. I felt much more confident with Craig by my side, but I wasn't looking forward to seeing Valerie's reaction when she found out we were still together. I knew that my life at school wouldn't be worth living — and Craig couldn't always be there to protect me.

I was tossing and turning in bed that night, going over and over it all in my head, when the answer suddenly came to me. I'd have to leave school.

I sat up straight, dislodging Jessie from her usual

bedtime spot on my feet. Why hadn't I thought of it before? I was miserable and couldn't concentrate on my work. It might be the best thing. I could get a job, I thought, go to night school for my A levels. People do.

My heart was thumping. It all made perfect sense. If I was working, I wouldn't have to see Valerie and her cronies every day. I wouldn't have to see them at all. I wouldn't have to see Anna, and be reminded of the way she'd let me down. I'd get a job of some sort, start earning real money . . . and swot and swot for my A levels at evening classes. It could be the answer to all my difficulties.

There was just one tiny little cloud on the horizon. I'd have to convince Mum and Dad.

"Leave school?" Dad said blankly, when I brought the subject up at breakfast the next morning. "But why?"

I hesitated. I didn't want to involve Dad, and more especially Mum, in the Valerie Maxwell saga. They had enough to worry about. I didn't even want them knowing that Mark's tragic story had come out, that people in town knew what had happened. It'd be enough to send poor Mum right over the edge. She'd suffered so much already, I couldn't risk doing that to her.

"I don't like it," I said, truthfully enough. "The – the girls are really unfriendly. Well, some of them. They've all known each other for years."

"But what about Anna?" said Mum. "I thought

you and she got on really well."

"We did. But . . . er . . . she's doing different courses, so I don't see much of her, and – and we had a bit of a row."

"You can't just walk out on your A level course because of some schoolgirl spat," said Dad impatiently, buttering another slice of toast. "I know what you kids are like – at daggers drawn one minute, best buddies the next. Don't worry, love, I'm sure it'll all blow over."

He doesn't understand, I thought. Even with Craig's love and support behind me, I was dreading Valerie finding out that we were still together.

"It's not that," I said, trying desperately to convince them I was serious without giving too much away. "I want to be out at work, earning money, not stuck at school like a little kid. I could do my A levels at evening classes if you want. Please, Dad!"

"Kerry, you're being ridiculous," Dad said crossly. "Wanting to leave school over some silly row – I won't hear of it! You've got your future to think about. I won't let you throw it away."

"But—"

"Did you hear what I said? Get on with your breakfast, and let's hear no more of this nonsense."

Anna wasn't in school that day, but Valerie was. She kept shooting glances across at me, but I ignored them. Just after lunch, I went into the cloakroom to fetch some tissues from my coat pocket and when I turned to leave, I saw Valerie standing in the doorway, Karen Connor and Judy Priestly behind her.

"Well?" Valerie said.

My heart began to thump. I couldn't push past all three of them, and there was no other way out of the cloakroom.

I didn't want them to know how scared I was.

"Well what?" I said.

"Still seeing Craig, are you?" said Valerie silkily.

I looked from her pretty, evil face to Judy's fat, pasty one and Karen's smug grin, and suddenly my fear fell away, to be replaced by anger. Who do they think they are, I thought, telling me who I can go out with? Making threats, trying to break Craig and me up?

"As a matter of fact, yes, I am," I said. "What's more, I'm going on seeing him. It's what I want, and it's what he wants, too. If you don't like it, it's just too bad. Now, would you let me past, please?"

I barged forward, past Valerie, in between Judy and Karen. Karen stumbled, Judy gasped, and Valerie caught hold of my arm.

"Get off me!" I yelled, giving her a shove. "Leave me alone!"

She shoved me back, Karen grabbed my other arm, and suddenly I was being pushed and pummelled between the three of them, Judy grabbing my hair and tugging it hard. I lashed out, lost my footing, staggered . . . and fell, hard, against one of the wooden lockers. Dazed, I tried to get up, and felt the toe of someone's platform shoe crash into my ribs. I heard a yell of pain and hardly realized it was me. Then all I could hear was running footsteps and then . . . silence.

"It's – Kerry, isn't it? Are you all right? What happened?"

It was Mrs Andrews, the school secretary, bending over me with a worried expression. I felt stunned and rather sick.

"I . . . must have fainted and hit my head," I muttered. Not for the world would I have told Mrs Andrews, or anyone on the staff, what had really happened. I could only imagine what Valerie and her cronies would do to anyone who grassed.

"You poor child! Come on, let me help you to the First Aid room. You're going to have a lovely black eye," fussed Mrs Andrews. "You'd better lie down for a while. Shall I phone your mother? Would she be able to collect you?"

"Er . . . I'm not sure. Dad might," I said, trying to remember whether Dad was on early or late shift today. As long as I didn't have to face Valerie again, I didn't care what happened to me.

I told Mum and Dad the same story I'd given Mrs Andrews, that I'd fainted and banged my head. Apart from an outsize headache, I didn't feel too bad once I got away from school, but what had happened had only convinced me that I had been right. Leaving school was the only option left to me. If I stayed, I'd be looking over my shoulder the whole time, waiting for Valerie's next move. I couldn't live like that; I wasn't even going to try.

Luckily, Mum and Dad went round to our neighbours that evening so I had a chance to call Craig and ask him to come round. I hobbled to the door to meet him like some old crock. He looked horrified when he saw me.

"What happened?" he asked.

"I got duffed up in the cloakroom," I said simply.

He flung his arms round me, making me flinch and cry out as he touched my bruised ribs.

"Oh love, I'm sorry,' he said wretchedly. "I – I didn't think. God, I could *kill* that Valerie Maxwell! Did you tell your parents about it?"

"How could I? If Mum finds out that people here know all about Mark. . . She's only just beginning to get better, Craig. But listen a moment."

"What?"

"I've had an idea – a brilliant idea that will solve everything."

He just looked at me blankly.

"Solve everything? But . . . how do you mean?"

"I'm going to leave school and get a job," I told him proudly.

"What?"

"Don't you see?" I said. "The only answer is for me to get away from Valerie altogether. If I don't, I'm not going to get a moment's peace. I'm going to be looking over my shoulder the whole time. That girl is mad – she'll stop at nothing. We've seen what she's capable of already, with her biker mate, and now this."

I shivered, remembering how scared I'd been as Valerie and the others had advanced towards me in the cloakroom. And there'd been the attack in Leeman Road. And the theft of my gold chain, the sabotaging of my sociology project, the bitchy remarks, the way she'd turned everyone against me. No, I *couldn't* stay at school.

Craig looked as though he didn't know what to say.

"But – what about your parents? What do they say? I mean, you're doing A levels and everything. Will they let you leave, just like that? Especially if you haven't been able to tell them why you want to?"

"We-ell," I admitted, "they weren't that keen, to be honest. But I'm sure I can talk them round. I mean, it's not like I'm dropping out altogether. I was planning to do A levels at night school or something."

Craig still looked uncertain.

"It's the only way," I urged him. "If I'm out at work, Valerie and her gang won't be able to touch me."

Craig put his arms round me again, much more gently this time, and buried his face in my hair.

"Oh Kerry!" he said roughly. "I – I don't know. I just want you to be safe, that's all. I can't believe this is happening, you know? How can Valerie be so vindictive? It's not as though she and I were ever that – well, you know. . ."

I shrugged. "She's a bitch," I said.

* * *

I didn't go to school for the rest of that week, telling Mum I still felt too sore and stiff, which was true. Craig rang me every single day, telling me he loved me, keeping my spirits up.

He's all I've got now, I thought. Craig – and Jessie. I haven't even got Anna.

I couldn't believe that it was all going to end, that I was going to walk out of the school gates one day and never go back, never see Valerie's spiteful face again. As for Mum and Dad, I'd have to convince them, somehow, that I was doing the right thing. After all, I reasoned, I was past school-leaving age. They couldn't drag me to school if I decided that I wanted to leave.

Perhaps if I fixed myself up with a job . . . then everyone would know I was serious.

I looked at the "Situations Vacant" column in the local paper, and made a note of a couple of employment agencies' numbers. There didn't seem to be much on offer for school leavers (except working in the chicken-processing factory, which sounded totally disgusting), but I told myself that something would turn up.

Now that I'd made my decision, I felt much better. I didn't care about being ignored at school, or about the way conversations suddenly seemed to stop when I walked into the common room. It didn't even hurt so much to see Anna turn and walk the other way when she saw me approaching. It served her right if she was on her own, I thought. I could never forgive her for what she'd done.

Soon, I thought. Soon, I'm going to get away from all this. Soon I would get a job. I'd still have Craig, and nothing else would matter.

It was on the following Saturday night that Craig dropped his bombshell. We'd arranged to meet in the pub and as soon as I arrived I could tell there was something wrong. He just wasn't his normal self.

It was my turn to buy the drinks, and when we were settled in a quiet corner I asked him what was the matter. Surely Valerie hadn't been making trouble again?

"What's wrong?" I asked.

Craig turned towards me and took both my hands in his. He looked absolutely desperate.

"Oh Kerry," he said, "I don't know how to tell you."

My heart started to thump painfully.

"Tell me what?" I was really frightened.

Craig took a deep breath. "Kerry," he said, "I'm going away."

I just stared at him, totally unable to speak.

"Going away?" I echoed.

"Yes. It's Carter's – you know, the garage I work for. They've got another branch in Cambridge and they're short-staffed there. They need a mechanic. Oh Kerry, I'm so sorry! I know it's an awful time. I tried to talk them out of it but they say I've got to go."

"Go to Cambridge," I repeated in a dazed voice. I just didn't seem able to take it in.

"Yes. For six months!"

Chapter 9

There was a strange roaring noise in my ears. I thought I might be going to faint.

"Kerry?" Craig was saying. "Kerry – listen. I'm sorry. Please, please say something!"

"You're going away," I repeated.

"Yes. But – but it's only for six months. I'll write to you every day, I promise. And – and I'll call you. And I'll be able to come home on Sundays, I expect."

"Sundays," I echoed.

"Yes. I – I have to work on Saturdays, I'm afraid."

I flung myself into his arms and burst into tears.

"Oh Craig!" I sobbed. "Don't go! I can't stand it if you go."

He held me tight. "I know. I wish . . . you don't know how much I wish I didn't have to. But the boss didn't give me any choice."

I sat back, shaking. I still couldn't believe it. If Craig went away, I would be completely alone. No boyfriend, no friends – and totally at the mercy of Valerie Maxwell and her cronies.

I shuddered. I could hardly bear to think about it.

"Craig," I said in a small voice, "can't I – why don't you let me come with you?"

He nearly choked on his beer. "Come with me? What d'you mean?"

"To – to Cambridge. You know I'm going to leave school anyway, and get a job. I'd have a much better chance of getting something in Cambridge than I would here."

Craig was still looking amazed – and, yes, horrified.

He doesn't want me to go with him, I thought miserably.

"But – but—" he began. "Kerry, how can you? I mean, what about your parents? And – and where would you live? And what sort of job would you get?"

"Anything," I said recklessly. "I don't care what I do – washing-up, scrubbing floors, anything. It couldn't be worse than being stuck here with Valerie Maxwell and without you!"

"But—"

"And where are you going to live, anyway?" I demanded. "We could get a flat somewhere – be together properly."

Craig looked wretched. "Carter's have fixed

something up for me already," he said. "There's a bedsit or something near the garage. I'll be sharing with another guy who works there."

"You don't want me," I whispered. "You don't want me to come with you, do you?"

Craig was silent. "It's not that," he said awkwardly. "Truly, it's not I – I love you, Kerry. You know I do. In some ways . . . well, there's nothing I'd like more than for us to be together. But it just isn't practical. Not right now, you must see that. Your parents'd go spare if you just took off to Cambridge with me, you know they would. And – and what about Jessie? You couldn't leave her, now could you?"

"You'll be leaving Chippy," I said sulkily.

"Dad and my brother are taking care of him. And it's only for six months, then I'll be back."

Six months! I thought. Six months of Valerie Maxwell. Six months of being stared at and ignored and called names and shoved around.

Six months of loneliness.

Six months of hell.

Craig and I left the pub in almost total silence. He tried to take my hand, but I pulled it away. All I could think was that he was deserting me, too.

"Please don't be like that, Kerry," he pleaded. "I don't want to leave you, you know I don't. I don't have any choice!"

"Yes, you do. You could tell your boss you're not

going. Tell him where to stick his stupid job," I snapped.

Craig was silent for a moment.

"Look," he said gently, "I know you're upset. I'm upset too. But we've got to be practical. What good would it do if I walked out of my job? There's not that much work round here for mechanics, or anyone else for that matter. You're talking about leaving school. OK. But what happens if you can't get work *and* I'm on the dole? I'm not scrounging off my dad."

Part of me knew that Craig was talking sense. He would be stupid to walk out of his job. And I knew there were going to be battles ahead once I told Mum and Dad I was definitely leaving school. I just didn't know which way to turn.

I squeezed Craig's hand remorsefully. None of this was his fault, and I couldn't bear the thought of losing him altogether.

He slipped his arm round my shoulders and swung me round to face him.

"It's going to be all right," he said firmly. "Hang on to that, Kerry. It's going to be all right, I promise."

I knew that the word would soon get around that Craig had gone to work in Cambridge. Just like Craig said – and Anna – when you live in a small town, everyone knows everyone else's business. Surprisingly, though, no one said anything to me at school about it. I was half-expecting some sarky comment from Valerie or one of her mob, but no one said a word. In fact, no one said anything to me at all.

I felt invisible. Totally invisible. Anna slunk out of the Sixth-Form room when I arrived. Simon and Paul just nodded coolly to me and went on with their conversation. Heather wasn't in. At one side of the room, Meg and Amy and Karen were discussing their weekend, with lots of shrieks and giggles and gasps of "He didn't!" and "What did you do then?". Some of the other guys were in a huddle talking about football.

No one even said "Hi, Kerry." No one asked me what sort of a weekend I'd had, or asked me how I'd got on with the English essay we'd been set, or offered me a coffee or a Coke from the machine. I just sat in one of the armchairs and read through my homework, trying to look as though I didn't notice that everyone was ignoring me, or that I didn't care. But I did. Of course I did.

When they *didn't* ignore me, it was worse.

At the end of Wednesday's Sociology lesson, Mr Perriman announced that the next project we'd be studying was, of all things, "Crime and Punishment".

"So I'd like you all to be thinking about the subject for a discussion next week," he told us, smiling pleasantly at us from behind his desk.

I could feel a blush simmering up the back of my neck as he spoke. Oh God! I thought. That's all I need. Crime and punishment.

Why, oh *why*, did that particular subject have to come up now? I could just imagine what Valerie would make of it. It was a perfect opportunity. . .

And I wasn't wrong. The moment Mr Perriman had left the room she got up and strolled ever-so-casually over to where I was sitting, putting my books away.

"Fancy that!" she said, smooth as silk. "A discussion on Crime and Punishment, eh? I bet you'll have lots to say about that, won't you?"

"Oh, shut up, Valerie," I muttered.

But she only raised her voice so that everyone could hear what she was saying.

"Should be an interesting discussion next week," she said. "After all, we've got someone in the class with personal experience, haven't we? I can't wait to hear what the killer's sister has to say."

Meg and Amy tittered.

To my horror I could feel tears springing to my eyes. I blinked them back hastily, not wanting Valerie to see me cry.

"Get lost!" I told her, my voice shaking.

She just smiled her malicious smile and strolled away, saying something to the others, who all looked over at me and burst out laughing.

I put my things together and hurried off home. That's it! I thought. I'm going to have another word with Mum and Dad tonight. I've got to make them understand. . .

However, that was easier said than done.

"We've had this conversation already, Kerry,"

Dad said in an exasperated voice. "You're not leaving school before A levels, and that's my final word."

"But I'd do them at night school," I protested desperately.

Mum was looking at me with a puzzled frown.

"I don't understand, Kerry," she said. "You seemed happy enough at that school earlier in the term. I know you're fed up about Craig going away, but you'll see him at the weekends, and anyway, it's not for ever, is it? What's the matter, love?"

I looked at her anxious face and Dad's stubborn one and it was all I could do not to burst into tears and tell them the whole truth – that there was someone at school who was making my life a complete misery. Someone who knew about Mark and the crash and who was never going to let me forget it.

If only I *could* tell them. Maybe they'd be able to help. . . But I knew, deep down, that I couldn't say anything – for Mum's sake. She was ever so much better. I hadn't heard her sobbing in the night for ages. Sometimes, she even managed to smile the way she used to. But she was still taking the tablets the doctor had given her and she still looked thin and white. Worrying about me, and about everyone knowing our family secret, was about the last thing she needed. No, I'd have to keep it to myself.

"Are you and Anna still not speaking?" Mum probed gently. "She doesn't seem to have called you for ages."

"No. No, we're not."

"Oh Kerry! Why don't you give her a ring? Whatever you fell out about, it can't be that important. Someone's got to be the first to say sorry."

I shook my head without a word.

"Well, it all seems like a lot of nonsense to me," Dad said impatiently. "Anna's a nice girl but I'm sure there are others you can team up with."

Oh, yes, sure, I thought. Judy Priestly. Meg Tate. Valerie Maxwell. What a choice!

"Anyway," Dad went on, "you're not leaving school, and that's that."

"But Dad—"

"Did you hear what I said?"

I knew, when Dad spoke in that tone of voice, that it was no use arguing with him. He was pretty easy-going as a rule, but once he put his foot down, that was it.

I was still just as determined to leave, though. Maybe, I thought, if I actually managed to fix myself up with a job, Dad would change his mind.

I sneaked into town in my free period the next day and went into our one-and-only employment agency.

"School leaver? Any experience?" said the snooty-looking girl behind the desk.

"Er . . . no," I admitted. "But I've got six GCSEs—"

"Can you use a word-processor? Ever worked in an office before?"

"Er . . . no."

"Sorry, the only vacancies we have are for people with experience."

But how was a person supposed to *get* experience, I thought crossly, if they were never even given a chance?

There weren't many junior vacancies advertised in the local paper, either. A trainee hairdresser's job, a junior receptionist, a couple of offers of part-time bar work and several mums wanting helpers. I rang one of those numbers but although the lady I spoke to was very nice, when I admitted that I had very little experience of looking after small children, she wasn't interested. The two pub jobs I rang up about were both taken.

That only left the chicken-processing factory on the industrial estate near where Dad worked, and I couldn't face that. I'd told Craig I was prepared to do anything, but the idea of pulling chickens' insides out, hour after hour . . . ugh! No thanks.

As I hurried back to school, I noticed that the town centre McDonald's was advertising for staff. Maybe I could work there. Then I remembered that Valerie and the others went in there practically every Saturday lunch-time, and sometimes in the week, too. I could just imagine what they'd say if they saw me behind the counter. I'd never hear the last of it.

No, I decided, my heart sinking. If I was going to get a job it would have to be further afield, somewhere I wasn't likely to run into any of my former schoolmates. Norwich, maybe. Or Cambridge. . .

Craig was as good as his word. I had a letter from him practically every day, and he phoned me as often as he could, too. He's one in a million, I thought. If it wasn't for him, I'd give up.

I just lived for Sundays, walking Chippy and Jessie if the weather was all right, going out in Craig's car if it wasn't. Even though everything else in my life was going horribly wrong, I still had Craig.

He made me tell him everything that Valerie and her gang had said and done.

"They haven't actually *done* anything much," I told him wearily. "It's more what they haven't done. They ignore me most of the time, and so does practically everyone else. If I come into the room, everyone shuts up, and then Valerie looks over my way and whispers something to the others and they all start giggling."

"Just try and ignore them. They'll get tired of it in the end," said Craig.

I dreaded going to school each day. Some days I made an excuse to Mum, and stayed at home. A tummy upset, period pains, earache – anything.

When I did go, I just concentrated on getting through the day as well as I could. No one spoke to me and I didn't speak to anyone, just kept my head down, and left as soon as I could in the evening. Now that it was dark at the end of the school day, I made sure I got the bus right outside the school gates. I wasn't going to chance walking home again, jumping every time I heard footsteps behind me. I was scared every time I found myself alone in a classroom, or in the cloakroom or canteen. I never knew when I'd find my way blocked by Valerie and the others, when they'd find an opportunity to have a go at me again.

I was really, really scared, even when they weren't doing anything, because I never knew what they were planning or what they might do next.

It happened on a Monday morning. For once, I was actually feeling quite cheerful as I went to school. Craig and I had had a really brilliant day together on the Sunday. It had been sunny, so we'd taken the dogs out, and Craig had given me a beautiful little brooch in the shape of a K that he said he'd bought in a local craft shop.

I wished I could've worn it to school, but I'd learned my lesson with Mark's gold chain. There was no way I was risking any more of my precious possessions, especially if Valerie got to know that Craig had given it to me.

No one said hello to me as I went into the Sixth-Form common room, but I was getting used to that. I made myself a cup of coffee and sat down to read through the English essay I'd written the night before.

Valerie was there. So were Karen and Judy. I saw them glance at one another and Judy smirked, but that was nothing new.

Paul and Simon came in. Paul actually said hi and Simon gave me a cool half-smile, which was better than nothing. Things had never been the same with those two after they'd accused me of spreading a rumour that they were gay, but I occasionally got the feeling they wouldn't mind being friends again – like today.

I smiled back encouragingly, but neither of them said anything.

I glanced at my watch and realized I had about three minutes before the bell went, so I went over to my locker to fetch my copy of *Henry V*.

It all happened in seconds.

I opened the locker. The first thing I noticed was a horrible, sickly smell. Then something rolled out of the locker and landed with a thump at my feet, splattering my shoes with blood – and worse.

I looked down. There, at my feet, was the body of a dead rat. Half its head seemed to be missing, as if it had either been run over by a car, or partly eaten by another animal.

I screamed – and screamed again.

"Oh God! Take it away! Get it away from me!"

I heard someone else – Simon? – call out my name. And then I fainted.

When I came round, I couldn't think where I was for a moment. Miss Latimer was beside me and I was in the school First Aid room.

"What happened, Kerry?" she asked me gently.

I didn't know what to say. If I told her I'd found a dead rat in my locker, I knew there would be the most almighty row, and the school would do their best to find out who had put it there. Oh, I knew, of course, but I wasn't telling. I could imagine what Valerie would do to the person who grassed on her.

"I – I fainted," I said.

"Yes, we know that. Simon Greaves and Heather Smith picked you up and then called me," she went on. "But what made you faint, Kerry? Aren't you well?"

"I'm – I'm all right," I muttered, though, as it happened, I felt terrible, shivery and sick. Every time I thought of that – that *thing*, I wanted to throw up.

Miss Latimer frowned. "This isn't the first time you've fainted at school, is it?" she said keenly. "Mrs Andrews told me she found you in the cloak-room not long ago."

"I'm all right," I repeated stubbornly.

Miss Latimer just looked at me.

Oh God! I thought. She knows something's wrong. I couldn't meet her eyes.

In the end, she just sighed.

"Well, Kerry," she said, "we've sent for your father and he's coming to pick you up and take you home. I shall suggest he takes you to the doctor to check out these fainting spells you keep having."

"Yes, Miss Latimer."

"Are you sure there's nothing you want to tell me? Perhaps I could help."

I looked away. "No, Miss Latimer," I said.

That's it, I thought. Whatever Dad or anyone says, I'm not coming back to school. Not *ever*.

As for Miss Latimer being able to help, there was no chance of that.

There was only one person who could help me now – Craig.

Mum had a hospital appointment the next morning, so it was easy for me to get away. I flung a few things into a bag any old how – jumpers, jeans, a couple of dresses, undies, my diary, favourite CDs. Jessie followed me around like a small brown shadow. I tried not to think about leaving her.

I wrote a letter to Mum and Dad, telling them they weren't to worry, that I was with Craig and everything was fine. I left it in the middle of their bed, where they couldn't miss it.

As I opened the door, I hesitated, and took one last look back. Jessie came running towards me, tail wagging hopefully. Tears sprang to my eyes.

"No, Jessie," I sobbed. "I – I'm sorry, I can't take you with me. Sit!"

Her tail drooped and she gave a pitiful little "wuff" of disappointment, then sat on the hall floor, looking the picture of dejection.

I brushed the tears from my eyes, picked up my bag, and walked out of the door.

* * *

"Kerry! What are you doing here?"

"Can – can I come in?" I said tiredly.

Craig looked amazed, but opened the door wider.

"Yes . . . yes, of course. What's happened?"

I flung my bag down on the shabby carpet and stumbled forward into his arms.

"Oh Craig!" I sobbed. "I – I've run away! I just couldn't stand it any more."

"Sssh! It's all right. Don't cry," said Craig tenderly. "Hush, Kerry. You're all right now. I'm going to make us both a cup of tea, and then you can tell me exactly what happened. Something has, hasn't it?"

I nodded forlornly, and sat down on the sagging sofa while Craig put the kettle on. I'd had a long, complicated journey on three different buses and it had taken me ages to find Craig's place.

He put a mug of strong tea into my shaking hands.

"There," he said. "That'll warm you up. Now, tell me what's happened."

I told him about the dead rat, shuddering even as I remembered it. I told him what Miss Latimer had said and how I'd vowed that I was never going back there.

Craig was silent for a moment. "You know," he said, "you should have told her."

I couldn't believe what I was hearing.

"Told her? You must be joking!" I snapped. "My

life wouldn't be worth living if Valerie knew I'd grassed on her. Simon and the others must've got rid of the – the *thing* before they called for help, or Miss Latimer would have put two and two together anyway. I'm sure she suspects that there's something going on."

"She probably does," he said. "It's time someone told her. Valerie Maxwell's got away with it for too long, because you're too scared to say anything."

"Do you blame me?" I gasped.

"No, not at all," said Craig. "All I'm saying is, enough is enough. Valerie depends on you being too scared to say anything. You've told me. You should tell your parents, too. And the school. And the police, even. Valerie's thumped you a couple of times and her friends have threatened me. She's got to be stopped."

"No," I said. "I – I can't face it, Craig. I just – I just want to stay here with you, out of her way. I never want to see her again."

Almost before I realized what was happening, I was in floods of tears again, and Craig was cradling me in his arms.

"All right, it's all right, love," he said tenderly. "Of course you can stay. You can sleep on the sofa. I don't suppose Dave will mind."

I had forgotten Craig shared the flat with another guy. I looked around.

"Where is he?" I asked.

"Down the pub. As usual," Craig grinned.

I didn't feel at all hungry, but Craig heated up a tin of tomato soup and made toast and I managed to swallow some. We sat together on the sofa watching TV with our arms round each other.

I was just beginning to feel a bit better when Craig said, "You know, Kerry, I really do think you should tell your mum and dad and let them deal with it."

I sat up abruptly. "Don't start that again," I snapped. "I thought you were on my side."

"I am," said Craig patiently. "I just think—"

There was a knock on the door.

"I wonder who that is?" said Craig. "Can't be the landlord, I paid him last week."

He went over and opened the door. I gave a gasp as I saw who was there, framed in the door-way.

My dad.

Chapter 10

"Kerry? Can we come in?" Dad said. I could see Mum standing behind him in the dimly-lit hall.

I sat down suddenly, feeling as though all the breath had been knocked out of me. My parents, here! I hadn't expected them to follow me. Were they very angry with me? What was going on?

Craig was looking as shocked as I was, but he seemed to recover first.

"C-come in, Mr Gilbert, Mrs Gilbert," he said awkwardly.

I saw Mum glance around her at the shabbiness of the surroundings and I bit my lip. I knew just what she must be thinking.

"Hello, Dad, Mum," I said feebly.

They sat down and just looked at me. Dad looked terrible. There were lines round his eyes that I could swear hadn't been there before and Mum was pale and ill-looking.

Oh God! I thought. I should've called them, let them know I was all right. I'd meant to, truly I had, but I'd been so miserable that I knew hearing their voices would just start me off crying again. What I'd been planning was to wait until I'd got a job, a *proper* job, and then to ring up and tell them I was fine and that everything was perfectly all right.

After all, I'd reasoned, Mum and Dad knew I hadn't been abducted or anything. They knew I was with Craig. They knew there wasn't anything to worry about – I'd told them so in my note. I'd told them I was determined to leave school and that I'd have a better chance of finding a job in Cambridge.

But now, looking at their worn, exhausted faces, I realized for the very first time how stupid I'd been, and how selfish. How could I possibly have thought they wouldn't worry?

"I don't know what to say to you," Dad said flatly.

I didn't know what to say either.

Craig jumped up. "I'll make us all a cup of tea," he said.

There was an awful silence.

"Mum. . ." I began.

"Why, Kerry?" she said. "Whatever the problem is why didn't you tell us? Couldn't you trust us? What sort of parents do you think we are, anyway? Did you imagine we were going to throw you out?"

"Throw me out?" I echoed, bewildered. "I – I don't understand."

Seeing my mum sitting there, looking tired and old, tears in her eyes, racked my heart with guilt and sorrow. I knew she was right. I should have told them what was going on. Why, why hadn't I? And what was all this about throwing me out?

"Kerry," Dad was saying, "you must have known that your mum and I would stand by you. You're all we've got, now."

Craig handed round mugs of tea. "I'm sorry," he said. "I was trying to persuade her to tell you. . ."

Dad gave him a scathing look. "Yes, well," he said, "what's done is done, I suppose. No use crying over spilt milk. And at least you're standing by her, facing up to your responsibilities like a man."

Craig looked puzzled. I looked from him to Mum and Dad and back to Craig again, not understanding what he meant. What was all this about Craig facing up to his responsibilities? What responsibilities?

An awful thought occurred to me. It sounded as though Mum and Dad had jumped to the wrong conclusion. It sounded as though they thought I was pregnant, and that was why I had run away!

"Dad, Mum," I said gently, "I'm not pregnant, you know."

Dad's jaw dropped, and I knew that I was right. That *was* what they'd thought, what they'd been afraid of. They'd been imagining that I was pregnant and that I had run off because I couldn't face telling them.

"She's not, honestly, Mr Gilbert," Craig reassured him.

"Not? But — but why — I don't understand. . ."

I heaved an enormous sigh. "Dad," I said, "you know I told you I wanted to leave school?"

"Oh — oh, yes, I remember. Some silly row you'd had with what's-her-name — Anna? But surely you wouldn't leave home over something as trivial as that?"

"You don't understand, Mr Gilbert," said Craig. "Kerry was having such a difficult time at school with this girl Valerie Maxwell, that she thought the only way out of it all was for her to get right away."

"But Kerry, you never said anything," Mum said doubtfully.

"I — I didn't want to worry you," I said. "Not after everything that had happened, with you being ill, and everything. Craig and I thought we could handle it ourselves. Only it just got worse and worse, and I — I just felt I had to get away."

"But what did she do?" Dad asked.

"She made Kerry's life a complete misery," said Craig angrily. "She's the leader of a little clique of girls and they ganged up on Kerry the whole time."

"You mean they bullied you," said Dad.

I hadn't ever actually thought of it like that, but when I did, I realized he was right. Valerie Maxwell was the school bully, no more and no less. Bullies aren't all great hulking blokes with their brains in their biceps.

"Tell us," said Dad gently.

So I told them. About Valerie being quite friendly at first, until she found out I wasn't going to be one of her adoring little circle of fans and hangers-on. And then, when she found out I was going out with Craig. . .

"She really had it in for me then," I told them. "The whole crowd of them did. They deliberately spilled coffee on my sociology project, they stole my gold chain that Mark gave me, they told Simon and Paul I'd been spreading rumours that they were gay, they wrote crude things about me on the blackboard, they called Mum names, they – they put a dead rat in my locker—"

"They attacked you in the street that time, too, didn't they?" Craig put in.

"Well, I couldn't swear it was them, but I'm pretty sure," I said.

Dad looked appalled. "They actually attacked you? Kerry, you should have gone to the police!" he snapped. "Schoolgirl pranks are one thing, but violence—"

"These weren't schoolgirl pranks," I said wearily. "One of Valerie's biker friends had a go at Craig in a pub car park, too. And – and then. . ."

"Then?" Mum prompted.

I bowed my head. "They – they found out about Mark," I whispered.

Mum didn't say anything but her face went even whiter.

"They – they started calling me names – you

know, stupid things like gangster's moll and killer's sister," I said. "She – Valerie said that if I didn't finish with Craig she'd make sure everyone in town knew what sort of family I came from. I was so scared, Dad. I didn't want anyone to know."

"But how did she find out about Mark?"

I shook my head. "Anna must have told her. I never told anyone else."

"Anna? But I thought she was your friend."

"So did I," I said bitterly. "That was why we fell out. I knew I could never trust her again, if she'd betray my secrets like that."

Mum and Dad were still looking stunned.

"And while all this was going on, you never said anything to us," Dad said.

"How could I? I – I didn't know where to turn, what to do. Mum had been so ill, so depressed, and you had so much else to worry you. When I came up with the idea of leaving, just getting right away, it seemed like the answer to all my problems."

Dad looked up at Craig.

"I owe you an apology, young man," he said awkwardly. "I'd been thinking – mind you, I still think you should have encouraged Kerry to tell someone in authority. Running away isn't the answer; you should have known that at your age."

"He did, Dad. He tried to persuade me to tell you – tell the school," I said.

There was another short silence.

"Well," Dad said, "the question is, what happens now?"

Craig and I looked at one another.

"I – I don't know," I whispered.

"Your English teacher came round when you didn't turn up at school," Mum put in.

"Miss Latimer?" I said, amazed. "But – but why?"

Dad sighed. "Oh, Kerry," he said, "did you think you could just disappear without anyone missing you or questions being asked? The school has been very concerned about you, you know. Anna's been on the phone, too. She sounded worried to death."

But I didn't want to think about Anna. If it hadn't been for her, a lot of this would never have happened. Why hadn't she kept her stupid mouth shut?

"We just didn't know what to think when we got your note," said Mum.

Every word she said made me feel more guilty. I've made a complete mess of everything, I thought.

"How did you find us?" Craig said.

"Through your parents, and Carter's Garage," said Dad. "Once we knew where you were, we just had to come and find out what was going on, whether you liked it or not."

"Oh Dad," I said, "I'm sorry. I never thought. . ."

Dad shrugged. "What we have to decide now", he repeated, "is what happens next. Craig, you'll go on working at this garage, here in Cambridge, won't you?"

Craig nodded.

"As for you, Kerry. . ."

My heart sank. I knew what Dad was going to say – that I'd have to go home. The awful thing was, I knew he was right. I could hardly stay here in this grotty flat with Craig and the unknown Dave, sleeping on the sofa. I *would* have to go home. But – home to what?

"They want you back at school, you know," said Mum.

"Back at school?" I echoed. "But. . ."

How could I possibly contemplate going back? Seeing Anna, Valerie and the others? Having it all start up again?

"Mum, I *can't*," I said desperately.

"That Valerie Maxwell will have to be sorted out," said Dad grimly. "I don't know what the school were thinking of, letting her get away with that kind of behaviour."

"They didn't know," I pointed out. "I didn't say anything – I couldn't. Valerie would've made things even worse for me if I'd grassed. She told me so."

"Then they *should* have known. Just like your mum and I should," said Dad remorselessly. "To think of all you went through, and we never noticed anything! I blame myself as much as you. Bullies thrive on secrecy, on people being afraid to speak out and no one else noticing, or saying anything if they do notice. I'll be in touch with Miss Latimer."

He must have seen how apprehensive I looked. I couldn't help being afraid of what would happen if it all came out into the open. What would Valerie do if I – if we – called her bluff?

"Kerry," Dad said, leaning forward, "we want you to come home. Mum, the school, even Jessie – all of us. Please."

I hesitated, looking at Craig.

"But. . ." I began uncertainly.

"It's up to you, Kerry," he said.

Mum and Dad and Craig and I talked and talked, far into the night.

I didn't want to leave Craig. In spite of the things Dad had said, I hated the idea of going back to school, even though I was beginning to see that my idea of getting a job and doing A levels at night school was a childish dream. If I wanted any kind of career, I needed those exams.

"I think you should go back," Craig said, after we'd talked round and round the subject for hours. "It's your future, after all. And it won't be the same now that your mum and dad know. There'll be things the school can do to deal with Valerie. You won't have to cope all alone. And I'll be home to see you on Sundays. Honestly, Kerry, it won't be nearly as bad as you think, you'll see."

I hugged him hard, thinking for about the millionth time how lucky I was to have Craig. He'd been there for me through the whole nightmare of the last few months. But whenever I thought of Valerie, I still felt sick. Sick and cold.

"I – I don't think I can face her . . . face them. . ." I faltered.

Craig squeezed my arm. "Yes, you can," he said encouragingly. "Your dad said he'd sort it, didn't he? So why don't you go home and see what happens?"

"I – I suppose I could. . ." I said. But I still wasn't sure.

When Dad opened the front door, Jessie shot down the path like a small, furry, brown bullet, her ridiculous little stump of a tail wagging so hard I thought it was going to wag right off. She jumped up at me, almost knocking me over. I dropped my bag in the confusion.

"Oh Jess, what a welcome!" I stammered.

Mum looked as though she might burst into tears at any moment, but she managed the sort of smile I hadn't seen on her face since Mark died.

"Welcome home, Kerry," she said.

We went in, our arms round each other, talking nineteen to the dozen, Jessie bounding around our heels. The house looked bright and welcoming and smelled of clean laundry and fresh coffee brewing.

I'm home! I thought gratefully. I'm really, really home.

Craig had promised me he'd be home for the weekend and reminded me that it was only five months until he'd be back for good. Everything was going to be all right for him and me – I knew it was. But I still had the rest of my life to sort out.

In the car, Dad had suggested asking Miss Latimer to come round after school one day soon, to have a chat with me.

"About. . .?" I prompted nervously.

"Well, about everything. About going back to school," said Mum. "It's going to be all right, you know, Kerry. Your dad and I will go up to the school tomorrow and see Miss Latimer and the Head."

"You'll tell them about Valerie Maxwell," I said nervously.

Mum nodded.

I didn't go in to school the next day, but Mum and Dad arranged their meeting with the Head straight away. They were gone for ages and I felt quite shaky when I saw the car draw up. What had happened? What had the Head said?

I made us all a cup of tea and Mum and Dad told me about the meeting.

"Apparently, the school is supposed to have an anti-bullying strategy in place, and when we told them what had happened to you they took it very seriously, said they'd have to review the whole situation," Dad said.

"And – and Valerie?"

Mum hesitated. "They'll be speaking to her, of course, but Miss Latimer will be able to tell you more about that when she comes over. Don't worry, Kerry. Your dad and I both want to make sure that your ordeal has ended and that no other student has to go through what you went through."

I shivered. Just thinking about Valerie and some of the things she'd done still made me feel cold inside. It does even now.

"Excluded?" I gasped.

Miss Latimer nodded.

"When we investigated, we found out that Valerie was very much the ringleader, as we thought. She led those other girls by the nose."

"Tell me about it!" I murmured. "Judy and Amy and Meg and the others always seemed to do exactly what she wanted."

"Yes," said Miss Latimer. "Valerie is a very strong character, with a lot of charisma and leadership qualities. Unfortunately, she chose to use them in a totally destructive way and we felt it better that she should continue her education elsewhere."

I could hardly believe it. Going back to school with no Valerie! No catty remarks, no sideways, spiteful looks, no giggling in corners, no threats . . . I could be friends with Simon and Paul and Heather and the others again. I could get on with my A levels.

"The whole school has had a talk and discussions about bullying and the problems it can cause," said Miss Latimer crisply. "We're determined that nothing like this will ever happen again, Kerry. We're very, very sorry that it had to happen at all, especially to a new student, and one who, like yourself, already had more than her fair share of problems to deal with."

I felt tears stinging the back of my eyes, but all I said was, "Thank you, Miss Latimer."

She got up to leave.

"So, we'll expect to see you at school on Monday morning as usual," she said with a smile.

I nodded. I'd always thought of her as really ancient, but when I looked closely, I realized she wasn't much older than Mum. And she'd actually *apologized* to me on behalf of the school. It wasn't all their fault, I knew that. Perhaps they should have taken more notice of what was going on, but I hadn't said anything either, had I? It had been like a conspiracy of silence. That was why Valerie had been able to get away with what she'd done. If any of us had said anything, it would've been different. And I couldn't believe I was the first and only person that Valerie Maxwell had bullied.

"I'll be there," I promised.

Walking through the school gates on Monday morning felt really, really strange. In some ways, it was like I'd never been away – everything looked just the same – but I knew everything had changed. I'd changed.

The first people I saw in the Sixth-Form block were Simon and Paul. They looked a bit embarrassed for a moment but then Simon squared his shoulders and came over to me.

"Kerry," he said warmly, "it's good to see you. I

177

– I'm sorry about what happened . . . you know. It was all a misunderstanding. . . ."

"It's OK," I said. "Forget it, why don't you? I just want to put the whole thing out of my mind, make a fresh start."

"We acted like wimps," said Paul. "We should've seen what Valerie was up to."

They both looked so shame-faced that I couldn't help smiling.

"I told you," I said. "Forget it!"

Simon squeezed my hand and just at that moment, Heather came in, her face breaking into a big smile when she saw me.

"Good to have you back, Kerry," was all she said. A few of the other Sixth-Formers came in, people I hardly knew. Even they smiled and said hi. They'd obviously taken the Head's pep talk seriously and were doing their best to make me feel at home, which was good.

When Karen and Judy and Meg came in, they scuttled over to the other side of the room, avoiding my eyes. I was busy sorting out my locker by then, so I didn't say anything to them. It was up to them to say sorry, I decided. I knew – I'd always known – that Valerie was the ringleader of their little gang, but it was hard for me to forgive the others, too. They'd made my life hell. Not one of them had thought for herself, bothered to find out the truth, questioned the bitchy things Valerie was saying about me. They'd just followed her like a bunch of sheep. I didn't think we could ever be friends.

As the bell rang for the start of morning school I suddenly realized there was someone missing.

Anna. I hadn't seen Anna.

She came into the common room at lunch-time, headed straight for me, and said, "Hello, Kerry."

"Hello," I said stonily.

Her freckled face was flushed and she was biting her lip anxiously. I remembered what Mum had told me, that Anna had rung up after I'd gone missing, asking for news.

"She was really worried about you, love," Mum had said. "I think she blamed herself—"

"So she should," I'd said stormily. "If she'd managed to keep her mouth shut instead of blabbing to Valerie . . . I *trusted* her, Mum!"

And now here she was, in front of me.

"Kerry," Anna said, "I want to tell you something."

"What?" I said ungraciously.

She swallowed hard.

"I want you to know that it wasn't me. I didn't tell Valerie about your brother. Honestly, it wasn't me."

I turned away. She'll have to do better than that, I thought, disappointed. Part of me longed to be friends with Anna, the way we used to be. I'd never admitted it, but I had missed her. But how could we be friends, after what had happened?

"You don't believe me, do you? You don't trust me," Anna cried, her mouth trembling.

I turned round again. Karen Connor and Meg

Tate were standing beside Anna.

"It's true, Kerry," said Karen in a small voice. "Anna never said anything."

"Then — then how did Valerie find out?" I demanded. "Anna was the only person I told."

"You know that weekend we all spent in London? When we went to Camden Lock and that? Well, Valerie met this really fit guy in a club."

I vaguely remembered them talking about it.

"And?" I said in a bored voice. I didn't see what this had to do with me, or Mark.

"He was a journalist," added Meg. "He was a reporter on one of the South London papers, in Sydenham or somewhere, and when we were all talking he was telling us about the cases he'd covered and, believe it or not, your brother's case came up. It was quite a high-profile case, he said — even made the *Evening Standard*."

I bowed my head. I remembered the lurid stories in the local press only too well. There had even been a tiny paragraph in the *Daily Mail*.

"Once Valerie knew it was your brother, she was all over him," said Meg. "I — I'm really sorry, Kerry. But you mustn't blame Anna. It had nothing to do with her at all."

I shook my head slowly, unable to meet Anna's eyes. It was an amazing, a horrific coincidence that Valerie had met someone who knew about Mark, but it wasn't that unlikely. As Meg said, it had been quite a high-profile story. And I'd blamed my best friend for betraying me!

It seemed that Simon and Paul, Karen and Meg and Judy – even Valerie herself, if she'd been here – weren't the only ones who needed to say sorry. I'd done my friend a terrible injustice. I'd jumped to conclusions and assumed that Valerie couldn't have found out any other way. Anna had sworn she hadn't betrayed my secret. Why hadn't I believed her?

"Did you know about this, Anna?" I asked her. She nodded.

"When – when you disappeared like that, after we'd had that row about it, I asked Judy and Meg and they told me how Valerie found out. I wanted to tell you, but", she shrugged, "you'd gone by then."

I closed my eyes. What an idiot I'd been! All I could do now was try to make it up to my former best friend.

"Anna," I said, "I'm so, so sorry, I can't tell you. I should've trusted you – should've listened to what you had to say instead of assuming the worst."

"Yes, you should," said Anna uncertainly. "You were ever so upset, I knew, but. . ."

We stood there, looking at one another. I was holding my breath. Would Anna be able to forgive me? Would she want to be friends again?

The bell rang.

Don't leave me in suspense, I thought desperately. School – well, *life* – just wouldn't be the same without Anna. I needed her, same as I needed Craig, and Mum and Dad, and even

Jessie. She was part of my life. If she still wanted to be.

"Anna. . ." I began.

"I've got to go. I've got a Physics practical," she said. "But – I'll see you after school, OK?"

She hurried away, but then she turned round and smiled, and I knew that everything was going to be all right.

Epilogue

I actually saw Valerie Maxwell again, a couple of months later. I'd been shopping in Norwich one Saturday afternoon, and was hurrying to meet Craig, who'd been at the match.

My heart skipped a beat when I saw her walking towards me. There she was, the girl who had done her best to split Craig and me up, separate me from my friends, make me give up my A level course, destroy my family. She'd almost ruined my life. Would have done if I'd let her.

I'd thought about her quite a lot since I'd been back at school. I'd imagined how I might feel if I ever saw her again, what I might say, or even do.

I won in the end, I thought. I had Craig, and my friends, and a future. What did Valerie have? She'd been kicked out of school, she'd lost her little clique of adoring fans, her status as the superstar of the Sixth Form, all the things that seemed to matter so much to her.

Valerie Maxwell, big-time loser. I wondered how she liked that?

I knew she had seen me. She caught my eye for a second and then hurriedly looked away. She was almost level with me now. . .

"Hello, Valerie," I said.

She stepped aside as if she was going to walk right past but I wasn't going to let her get away with that. I caught her arm.

"Just a minute," I said.

"What do you want?" she muttered.

One or two passers-by looked at us curiously, but I didn't care.

"Just to tell you what I think of you, you spiteful, lying bully," I said. "You did your best to wreck my life, just because you wanted to get your claws into my boyfriend again. Well, you didn't make it, did you? You're a failure . . . and a loser . . . and now everyone knows it. Even you!"

I didn't bother to keep my voice down. People were staring.

"That's it, gel! You tell 'er!" said a fat, red-faced farmer.

Valerie was actually *blushing*! I wouldn't have believed it if I hadn't seen it with my own eyes. I felt about twenty feet tall.

"You got what was coming to you in the end, didn't you?" I sneered.

"I – I –" she stammered.

I'd never seen Valerie lost for words before. She looked . . . smaller, somehow, without her adoring crowd of hangers-on. Small and sort of lonely. Even her hair seemed to have lost some of its shine. She looked pathetic.

"You're pathetic," I told her, as I turned away.

It was like a weight lifting from my heart when I realized that Valerie Maxwell couldn't frighten me any more. I didn't care what she said, what she thought, how she felt. She just didn't matter. She'd lost her power to hurt me long ago.

A few seconds later she had disappeared into the crowd. And, just across the road, I could see Craig waiting for me.

Point Romance

Are you burning with passion, and aching with desire? Then these are the books for you! Point Romance brings you passion, romance, heartache ... and *love*.

Forget Me Not:
Lavender Blue
Lorna Read

Silver Rose
Jill Eckersley

The White Cockade
Janis Dawson

The Wildest Dream
Kirsty White

The Druid Stone
Helen McCann

First Comes Love:
Till Death Us Do Part
Last Summer, First Love:
A Time to Love
Goodbye to Love
Jennifer Baker

A Winter Love Story
Malibu Summer
Winter Love, Winter Wishes
Jane Claypool Miner

Two Weeks in Paradise
Spotlight on Love
Love Letters
Denise Colby

Summer Nights
New Year's Eve
Last Dance
Saturday Night
Caroline B. Cooney

Cradle Snatcher
Kiss Me Stupid
Alison Creaghan

Breaking Away
Jill Eckersley

Two Timer
Love Triangle
Lorna Read

Summer Dreams, Winter Love
Mary Francis Shura

French Kiss
Russian Nights
Crazy About You
Ice Hot!
Can't Buy Me Love
Robyn Turner

Hopelessly Devoted
Dream Ticket 1: Blazing Kisses
Dream Ticket 2: Freezing Heart
Dream Ticket 3: Follow the Sun
Amber Vane

Shy Boy
Kirsty White